CHARLOTTE

CHARLOTTE

DAVID FOENKINOS

Translated from the French by Sam Taylor

CANONGATE

Published in Great Britain in 2017 by
Canongate Books Ltd, 14 High Street, Edinburgh EH1 1TE

www.canongate.co.uk

1

This edition first published in the United States in 2016 by
The Overlook Press, Peter Mayer Publishers, Inc.
141 Wooster Street, New York NY 10012

British Library Cataloguing-in-Publication Data
A catalogue record for this book is available on
request from the British Library

ISBN 978 1 78211 794 0

Book design and type formatting by Bernard Schleifer

Printed and bound in Great Britain by Clays Ltd, St Ives plc.

Anyone who cannot come to terms with his life while he is alive needs one hand to ward off a little his despair over his fate.

—FRANZ KAFKA, *Diary*

This novel is inspired by the life of Charlotte Salomon.
A German painter murdered at the age of twenty-six,
    when she was pregnant.
My principal source is her autobiographical work,
    Life? or Theater?

Part One

1

Charlotte learned to read her name on a gravestone.

So she wasn't the first Charlotte.
Before her, there had been her aunt, her mother's sister.
The two sisters were very close, until one evening in November 1913.
Franziska and Charlotte sing together, dance and laugh together.
But never to excess.
There is always a reserve to their displays of happiness.
Perhaps this is linked to their father's personality.
An intellectual, strict and unyielding, with an interest in art and antiques.
For him, nothing could be more fascinating than a handful of Roman dust.
Their mother is gentler.
But it is a gentleness tinged with sorrow.
Her life has been a series of tragedies.
But more on that later.

For now, let's talk about Charlotte.
The first Charlotte.
She is beautiful, with long dark hair like a promise.
It all begins with the slowness.
Little by little, she does everything more slowly: eating, walking, reading.
Something inside her is slowing down.
Her body, I imagine, being infiltrated by melancholy.
The kind of melancholy that devastates, that never goes away.
Happiness becomes an island in the past, unreachable.

But nobody notices the arrival of this slowness in Charlotte.
It is insidious.
People compare the two sisters.
One simply smiles more than the other.
At most, someone might remark the occasional daydream that goes on
    too long.
But night is taking over her.
The night she must wait for, so that it can be her last.

It is such a cold November night.
While everyone else is sleeping, Charlotte gets out of bed.
She gathers a few belongings, as if she's going on a trip.
The city seems at a standstill, frozen in this early winter.
Charlotte has just turned eighteen.
She walks quickly toward her destination.
A bridge.
A bridge she loves.
The secret locus of her darkness.
She has known for a long time that it will be the last bridge.
In the black night, unseen, she jumps.
Without the slightest hesitation.
She falls into the icy water, her death an ordeal.

Her body is found early the next morning, washed up on a riverbank.
Completely blue in places.
Her parents and her sister are woken by the news.
The father is paralyzed, utterly silent.
The sister weeps.
The mother howls with pain.

The next day's newspapers run stories about this girl.
Who took her own life without any explanation.

And perhaps that is the ultimate outrage.
Violence added to violence.
Why?
Her sister considers this suicide an affront to their closeness.
Mostly, she feels responsible.
She never saw, never understood that slowness.
Now she moves forward, with guilt in her heart.

2

The parents and the sister do not attend the funeral.
Devastated, they shut themselves away.
They probably feel a little ashamed too.
They flee the eyes of others.

A few months pass like this.
In the impossibility of taking part in the world.
A long period of silence.
To speak is to risk mentioning Charlotte.
She hides in wait behind every word.
Silence is the survivors' only crutch.
Until the moment when Franziska touches the piano.
She plays something, sings softly.
Her parents move over to her.
Surprised by this manifestation of life.

The country enters the war, and perhaps this is for the best.
Chaos is the perfect backdrop to their pain.
For the first time, the conflict is global.
Sarajevo brings the fall of the old empires.

Millions of men rush to their deaths.

The future is fought over in long tunnels dug in the earth.

Franziska decides to become a nurse.

She wants to heal the wounded, cure the sick, bring the dead back to life.

And to feel useful, of course.

This girl who lives each day with the feeling of having been useless.

Her mother is horrified by this decision.

It gives rise to tensions and arguments.

A war within the war.

But it makes no difference: Franziska signs up.

And finds herself near the danger zone.

Some think her brave.

But she is quite simply no longer afraid of death.

In the heat of battle, she meets Albert Salomon.

He is one of the youngest surgeons.

He is very tall and very concentrated.

One of those men who seem in a rush even when they are still.

He manages a makeshift hospital.

On the front, in France.

His parents are dead, so medicine is his only family.

Obsessed with his work, nothing can distract him from his mission.

He shows little attention to women.

Barely even registers the presence of a new nurse.

She smiles at him constantly, all the same.

Thankfully, something happens to change this.

In the middle of an operation, Albert sneezes.

His nose runs, he needs to blow it.

But his hands are deep in a soldier's guts.

So Franziska approaches with a handkerchief.

It is at this very moment that he finally looks at her.

. . .

One year later, Albert takes his courage in his hands.

His surgeon's hands.

He goes to see Franziska's parents.

They are so cold that he loses his nerve.

Why has he come here?

Oh yes . . . to ask for their daughter's . . . hand in . . . marriage . . .

To ask for what? the father grumbles.

He doesn't want this gangly beanpole for a son-in-law.

He's not good enough to marry a Grunwald!

But Franziska insists.

She says she is deeply in love.

It's hard to be sure.

But she is not the type for passing whims and fancies.

Since Charlotte's death, life has been reduced to its essentials.

The parents finally give in.

They force themselves to rejoice a little bit.

To learn to smile again.

They even buy flowers.

It has been so long since colors were seen in their living room.

Somehow they are reborn through the petals.

At the wedding, though, they look like mourners.

3

Right from the beginning, Franziska is left alone.

Is this really *married life*?

Albert returns to the front.

The war is mired in mud, it seems endless.

One vast slaughter in the trenches.
Just don't let her husband be killed.
She does not want to be a widow.
She's already a . . .
Actually, what is the word for someone who has lost a sister?
There is no word.
Sometimes the dictionary says nothing.
Frightened by pain, just like her.

The young newlywed wanders around her large apartment.
On the second floor of a bourgeois building in Charlottenburg.
Charlotte town.
It is located at 15 Wielandstrasse, near the Savignyplatz.
I have often walked that street.
Even before I knew about Charlotte, I loved her neighborhood.
In 2004, I wanted to entitle a novel "Savignyplatz."
That name resonated strangely within me.
Something drew me to it, though I didn't know why.

A long hallway runs through the apartment.
Franziska often sits there to read.
In the hallway, she feels as if she is at the border of her home.
Today, she closes her book quite quickly.
Feeling dizzy, she heads to the bathroom.
And splashes some water on her face.
It takes her only a few seconds to understand.

While caring for a wounded man, Albert receives a letter.
Seeing his face turn pale, a nurse becomes worried.
My wife is pregnant, he finally sighs.
In the months that follow, he tries to return to Berlin as often as possible.

But most of the time, Franziska is alone with her belly.
She walks along the hallway, already speaking to her child.
So desperate to put an end to her solitude.
Deliverance comes on April 16, 1917.
It is the first appearance of a heroine.
But also of a baby that cries constantly.
As if she refused to accept her birth.

Franziska wants to call her Charlotte, in homage to her sister.
Albert does not want his daughter to bear a dead woman's name.
Still less one who committed suicide.
Franziska weeps, outraged, infuriated.
It is a way of making her live again, she thinks.
Please, Albert begs, be reasonable.
But he knows that she isn't.
It is part of why he loves her, this gentle madness.
This way she has of never being the same woman.
She is by turns free and submissive, feverish and dazzling.
He senses that conflict is pointless.
Besides, who ever feels like fighting during a war?
So Charlotte it will be.

4

What are Charlotte's first memories?
Smells or colors?
More likely, they are notes.
The tunes sung by her mother.
Franziska has an angel's voice and she plays piano too.
From her first days of life, Charlotte is soothed by this.

Later, she will turn the pages of sheet music.
And so her early years pass, enveloped in melody.

Franziska likes going for walks with her daughter.
She takes her to Berlin's green heart, the Tiergarten.
A small island of peace in a city still sunk in defeat.
Little Charlotte observes the damaged, mutilated bodies.
She is scared by all these hands reaching out toward her.
An army of beggars.
She lowers her eyes to avoid seeing their broken faces.
And does not look up again until she is in the woods.
There, she can run after the squirrels.

Afterward, they must go to the cemetery.
So they never forget.
Charlotte understands early that the dead are part of life.
She touches her mother's tears.
This mother who mourns her dead sister as she did on the day of her death.
Some sorrows never pass.
On the gravestone, Charlotte reads her name.
She wants to know what happened.
Her aunt drowned.
Didn't she know how to swim?
It was an accident.
Franziska quickly changes the subject.
And so comes the first arrangement with reality.
The play begins.

Albert disapproves of these trips to the cemetery.
Why do you take Charlotte there so often?
It's a morbid attraction.

He asks her to visit less frequently, not to take their daughter.
But how can he know if she obeys?
He is never there.
He thinks of nothing but his work, say his parents-in-law.
Albert wants to become the greatest doctor in Germany.
When he is not in the hospital, he spends his time studying.

Never trust a man who works too much.
What is he seeking to avoid?
Fear, or simply a feeling.
His wife's behavior is increasingly unstable.
She seems absent at times, he notices.
As if she were taking a vacation from herself.
He tells himself she's a daydreamer.
Often we try to find pleasant reasons for other people's strangeness.
In the end, the way she acts becomes worrying.
She lies in bed for days on end.
She doesn't even pick Charlotte up from school.

And then, suddenly, she becomes herself again.
In the space of a minute, she snaps out of her lethargy.
Without the slightest transition, she starts taking Charlotte everywhere.
Into town, to the park, to the zoo and museums.
They must walk, read, play piano, sing, learn all there is to learn.
In lively moments, she likes organizing parties.
She wants to see people.
Albert loves those soirées.
They are his deliverance.
Franziska sits at the piano.
It's so beautiful, that way she has of moving her lips.
As if she were conversing with the notes.

For Charlotte, her mother's voice is a caress.
When you have a mother who sings like that, nothing bad can happen to you.

Like a doll, Charlotte stands up straight in the middle of the living room.
She greets the guests with her brightest smile.
The smile she worked on with her mother, until her jaw ached.
Where is the logic?
Her mother shuts herself up for weeks at a time.
Then, suddenly, the social demon possesses her.
Charlotte enjoys these transformations.
She prefers anything to apathy.
A deluge is better than a drought.
But the drought returns now.
The rain of life ceases as abruptly as it started.
And once again, Franziska lies in bed, exhausted by nothing.
Lost in contemplation of some other world at the far end of her room.

Faced with her mother's mood swings, Charlotte is docile.
She tames her melancholy.
Is this how one becomes an artist?
By growing accustomed to the madness of others?

5

Charlotte is eight when her mother's state worsens.
The depressive phases drag on.
She no longer has any desire to do anything, feels useless.
Albert implores his wife.
But the darkness is already settled in their bed.
I need you, he says.

Charlotte needs you, he says.
She falls asleep, for the night.

But gets up again.
Albert opens his eyes, watches her.
Franziska walks over to the window.
I want to see the heavens, she says to reassure her husband.
Often, she tells Charlotte that everything is more beautiful in heaven.
And adds: when I'm there, I'll send you a letter to tell you all about it.
The afterlife becomes an obsession.
Don't you want mama to become an angel?
Wouldn't that be wonderful?
Charlotte says nothing.

An angel.
Franziska knows one: her sister.
Who had the courage to put an end to it all.
To exit life silently, without warning.
The death of an eighteen-year-old girl.
The death of promise.
Franziska believes there is a hierarchy of horror.
The suicide of a mother is a superior suicide.
She could occupy first place in the family tragedy.
Who would contest the supremacy of her devastation?

One night, she gets quietly out of bed.
Not even breathing.
For once, Albert does not hear her.
She goes to the bathroom.
Picks up a vial of opium and swallows it all.
Her groan finally awakens her husband.

He rushes over, but the door is locked.
Franziska does not open it.
Her throat is on fire, the pain is unbearable.
She doesn't die, however.
And her husband's panic ruins her goodbyes.

Does Charlotte hear all this?
Does she wake up?
In the end, Albert manages to open the door.
He brings his wife back to life.
The dose was too small.
But now he knows.
Death is no longer merely a fantasy.

6

When she wakes up, Charlotte goes in search of her mother.
Your mama was sick in the night.
You mustn't disturb her.
For the first time, the little girl goes to school without seeing her.
Without kissing her.

Franziska will be safer at her parents' house.
That is what Albert thinks.
If she stays alone, she will kill herself.
It is impossible to reason with her.
Franziska goes back to her old bedroom.
The place where she grew up.
The place where she was happy with her sister.
With her parents' support, she regains a little strength.

Her mother tries to conceal her anxiety.
How is it possible?
Her second daughter attempting suicide, after the first killed herself.
No hope of any respite.
She seeks help wherever she can.
They call a neurologist, a family friend.
She has gone through a rough patch, but it will pass, he reassures them.
An excess of emotion, a highly sensitive personality, nothing more.

Charlotte worries.
Where is mama?
She is sick.
She has flu.
It's very contagious.
So it's better not to see her for the moment.
She'll be back soon, Albert promises.
Though he doesn't sound altogether convincing.
He is angry with his wife.
Especially when he sees Charlotte in such distress.

All the same, he visits her every evening.
His parents-in-law greet him coldly.
They hold him responsible.
He is never at home, always working.
The suicide attempt is obviously an act of despair.
Provoked by her terrible loneliness.
They have to blame someone.
And what about your other daughter, he wants to shout, is that my fault too?
But Albert remains silent.
He ignores them, and goes to sit next to the bed.
Alone with his wife at last, he brings up a few memories.

It always ends like this, with memories.
For a moment, things look hopeful.
Franziska takes her husband's hand, manages a faint smile.
These are instants of peace, even of tenderness.
Brief passages of life between the dark desires.

They choose a nurse to care for the patient.
That is the official version.
Her real job, of course, is to watch over Franziska.
The days pass under the gaze of this stranger.
Franziska never asks about her daughter.
Charlotte no longer exists.
When Albert brings one of their daughter's drawings, the mother turns her
    face away.

7

The Grunwalds eat in the large dining room.
The nurse crosses the room, sits down next to them for a moment.
Suddenly, the mother is seized by a vision.
Franziska alone in her room, walking over to the window.
She glares at the nurse.
Jumps to her feet and runs upstairs to her daughter.
She opens the door, just in time to see the body falling.
She screams her head off, but it's too late.
A thud.
The mother moves forward, trembling.
Franziska is lying in a pool of her own blood.

Part Two

1

When she hears the news, Charlotte says nothing.
A violent attack of flu has taken her mother.
She thinks about that word: flu.
One word and it's all over.
Years later, she will finally learn the truth.
In an atmosphere of general chaos.

For now, she comforts her father.
It's all right, she says.
Mama told me about this.
She has become an angel.
She always said how wonderful it is in heaven.
Albert does not know how to respond.
He wants to believe this too.
But he knows the truth.
His wife has left him.
Alone, with their daughter.

Everywhere he goes, memories haunt him.
In every room, through every object, she is there.
The air in the apartment is the same air she breathed.
He wants to rearrange the furniture, smash it all up.
Or, better still, move to a new house.
But when he speaks to Charlotte about this, she refuses.
Her mother promised to send her a letter.

Once she is up in heaven.

So they have to stay here.

Otherwise mama won't be able to find us, says the little girl.

Each evening, she waits for hours.

Sitting on the window ledge.

The horizon is dark, gloomy.

Perhaps that is why her mother's letter has not found its way here.

Days pass, without any news.

Charlotte wants to go to the cemetery.

She knows every inch of it.

She walks up to her mother's gravestone.

Don't forget your promise: you have to tell me everything.

But still nothing.

Nothing.

This silence, she can't stand it anymore.

Her father tries to reason with her.

The dead cannot write to the living.

And it's better that way.

Your mother is happy, up there.

There are lots of pianos hidden in the clouds.

What he says doesn't make much sense.

His thoughts get tangled up.

Finally, Charlotte understands there will be no letter.

She is terribly angry with her mother.

2

Now, it is time to learn solitude.

Charlotte does not share his feelings.

Her father hides in his work, buries himself in it.
Every evening, he sits at his desk.
Charlotte watches him, stooped over his books.
Piles of books, high as towers.
Mad-eyed, he mumbles all sorts of formulas.
Nothing can block his progress on the path to knowledge.
Nor on the path to renown.
He has just been given a professorship at the medical faculty in Berlin.
It is a consecration, a dream.
Charlotte does not seem very happy about it.
In truth, it has become difficult for her to express any emotion.

At the Fürstin-Bismarck school, people whisper as she passes.
They must be kind to her, her mama is dead.
Her mama is dead, her mama is dead, her mama is dead.
Thankfully, the building is comforting, with its wide stairways.
A place where pain is soothed.
Charlotte is happy to go there every day.
I took the same walk myself.
Many times, following in her footsteps.
There and back, in search of Charlotte as a child.

One day, I went inside the school.
Girls were running through the lobby.
I thought that Charlotte could still be among them.
At the front office, I was welcomed by the academic counselor.
A very affable woman named Gerlinde.
I explained to her the reason I was there.
She did not seem surprised.
Charlotte Salomon, she repeated to herself.
We know who she is, of course.

. . .

So began a long visit.

Meticulous, because every detail matters.

Gerlinde talked up the virtues of the school.

Observing my reactions, my emotions.

But the most important was yet to come.

She suggested I go to see the biology equipment.

Why?

Because none of it has changed.

It is like diving into the last century.

Diving into Charlotte's world.

We walked through a dark, dusty corridor.

And came to an attic full of stuffed animals.

And insects spending eternity inside a jar.

A skeleton caught my eye.

Death, the ceaseless refrain of my quest.

Charlotte must have studied it, Gerlinde announced.

I was there, almost a century after my heroine.

Analyzing, in my turn, the form of a human body.

At the end, we visited the beautiful auditorium.

A group of girls was posing for the class photo.

Encouraged by the photographer, they were goofing around.

A successful attempt to immortalize the joy of living.

I thought of Charlotte's class photo, which I had seen before.

It was not taken in this room, but in the schoolyard outside.

It is a deeply disturbing picture.

All the girls stare into the lens.

All of them, but one.

Charlotte's eyes are turned in a different direction.

What is she looking at?

3

Charlotte lives with her grandparents for a while.
She stays in her mother's childhood bedroom.
This confuses the grandmother.
She gets her eras mixed up.
A child with the face of her first daughter.
A child with the same name as her second.
In the night, fearful, she gets up several times.
She has to check that little Charlotte is sleeping peacefully.

The girl grows wild.
Her father hires nannies and she does all she can to drive them to despair.
She hates anyone who tries to take care of her.
Worst of the bunch: Miss Stagard.
A stupid, vulgar woman.
Charlotte is the most badly brought-up girl she has ever known, she says.
Thankfully, on an outing one day, she falls into a crevasse.
She screams with pain, her leg broken.
Charlotte is in seventh heaven, finally rid of her.

But with Hase, everything is different.
Charlotte loves her instantly.
As Albert is never home, Hase practically lives there.
When she washes, Charlotte gets up to spy on her.
She is fascinated by the size of her breasts.
It is the first time she has seen such big ones.
Her mother's were small.
What about hers: what will they be like?

She would like to know what is preferable.

On the apartment landing she sees a neighbor boy her own age, and
    asks him.

He seems very surprised.

Then finally answers: large breasts.

So Hase is lucky, but she isn't very pretty.

Her face is a little puffy.

And she has hairs on her upper lip.

In fact, you could probably call it a moustache.

So Charlotte goes back to see her neighbor.

Is it better to have large breasts and a moustache . . .

Or small breasts with the face of an angel?

The boy hesitates again.

In a serious voice, he replies that the second solution seems better to him.

Then he walks away without another word.

After that, he will always be embarrassed when he sees the strange girl
    next door.

As for Charlotte, she feels relieved by this response.

Deep down, she is pleased that men do not like Hase.

She loves her too much to risk losing her.

She doesn't want anyone to love her.

Nobody but her.

4

It is the first Christmas without her mother.

Her grandparents are there, colder than ever.

The Christmas tree is immense, too big for the living room.

Albert bought the biggest and most beautiful one he could find.

For his daughter, naturally, but also in memory of his wife.
Franziska adored Christmas.
She would spend hours decorating the tree.
It was the highlight of her year.
The tree is dark now.
As if it, too, were in mourning.

Charlotte opens her presents.
They are watching her, so she plays the role of the happy girl.
A little theater to lighten the moment.
To dispel her father's sadness.
Silence is what hurts most of all.
At Christmas, her mother used to sit at the piano for hours.
She loved Christian hymns.
Now the evening passes without a single melody.

Charlotte often looks at the piano.
She is incapable of touching it.
She can still see her mother's fingers on the keyboard.
On this instrument, the past is alive.
Charlotte has the feeling that the piano can understand her.
And share her wound.
The piano is like her: an orphan.
Every day, she stares at the open sheet music.
The last piece her mother ever played.
A Bach concerto.

Several Christmases will pass this way, in silence.

5

It is now 1930.

Charlotte is a teenager.

People like to say that she is *in her own world*.

Being *in one's own world*, where does that lead?

To daydreams and poetry, undoubtedly.

But also to a strange mix of disgust and bliss.

Charlotte can smile and suffer at the same time.

Only Hase understands her, and it happens without words.

In silence, Charlotte rests her head on the nanny's chest.

Like that, she feels listened to.

Some bodies are consolations.

But Hase no longer spends so much time looking after Charlotte.

Albert says a thirteen-year-old girl has no need for a nanny.

Does he have any idea what his daughter wants?

If that's how it is, she refuses to grow up.

Charlotte feels ever more alone.

Her best friend is now spending more time with Kathrin.

A new pupil in the school, and already so popular.

How does she do it?

Some girls have the gift of making others love them.

Charlotte is afraid of being abandoned.

The best solution is to avoid becoming attached.

Because nothing lasts.

She must protect herself from potential disappointments.

But no, that's ridiculous.

She can see what's happening to her father.
By separating himself from other people, he has become a gray man.
So she encourages him to go out.

During one dinner party, he finds himself talking to a famous opera singer.
She has just made a record, and it's wonderful.
All over Europe, people are praising it.
She also sings in churches: sacred music.
Albert is tongue-tied, intimidated.
The conversation is full of silences.
If only she was ill, the doctor would know what to say.
Alas, this woman is in sickeningly good health.
After a while, he stammers that he has a daughter.
Paula (that's her name) is charmed by this.

Chased constantly by admirers, she dreams of a man who is not an artist.
Kurt Singer, the dashing Opera House director, idolizes her.
He wants to give up everything for her (his wife, in other words).
His wooing borders on harassment.
For months, he has been promising Paula the earth.
A neurologist too, he helps women with nervous problems.
To cast a spell on her, he even tries hypnosis.
Paula starts to yield, then pushes him away.

One night, coming out of a concert, Kurt's wife suddenly appears.
Desperate, she throws a vial of poison at Paula.
Poison that she probably thought about swallowing.
A tragic love story.
This incident leaves Paula weak.
She decides it is time she got married.
To put an end to this exhausting situation.

In this context, Albert seems to her like a refuge.
Anyway, she prefers the surgeon's hands.

Albert tells Charlotte about his meeting with Paula.
Thrilled, she insists that he invite her to dinner.
It would be such an honor.
He obeys.
On the evening in question, Charlotte wears her best dress.
The only one she likes, in truth.
She helps Hase prepare the table and the meal.
Everything must be perfect.
At eight o'clock, the doorbell rings.
Eagerly, she rushes to open it.
Paula gives her a big smile.
You must be Charlotte, says the opera singer.
Yes, that's me, she wants to reply.
But no sound emerges.

The meal passes in an atmosphere of muted joy.
Paula invites Charlotte to see her in concert.
And afterward, you can visit my dressing room.
You'll see, it's very beautiful, Paula adds.
Backstage is the only place where the truth exists.
She speaks softly, her voice so fine.
There is nothing diva-like about her.
On the contrary, there is a delicacy to her gestures.
Everything is going wonderfully, thinks Albert.
It's as if Paula had always lived here.

After dinner, they beg her to sing.
She approaches the piano.

Charlotte's heart is no longer beating—it is pounding.
Paula leafs through the sheet music next to the piano.
Finally she chooses a Schubert lied.
And places it over the Bach.

6

Charlotte cuts out every article about Paula.
It fascinates her, that one person can be so loved.
She loves hearing the applause in the concert hall.
She is proud that she knows the artist *personally*.
Charlotte basks in the audience's enthusiasm.
The noise of admiration is fabulous.
Paula shares with her the love she receives.
She shows Charlotte the flowers and the letters.
All of this takes the form of a strange consolation.

Life becomes richer, goes faster.
Suddenly everything seems frenetic.
Albert asks his daughter what she thinks of Paula.
I simply adore her.
Well, that's perfect, because we've decided to get married.
Charlotte throws her arms round her father's neck.
Something she hasn't done for years.

The wedding takes place in a synagogue.
Raised by her rabbi father, Paula is a true believer.
Judaism has had little importance in Charlotte's life.
One might even say: none at all.
Her childhood is based around *an absence of Jewish culture*.

In the words of Walter Benjamin.
Her parents lived a secular life.
And her mother loved Christian hymns.
At thirteen, Charlotte is discovering this world that is supposedly hers.
She observes it with that easy curiosity we have for things that seem
    distant to us.

7

Albert's new wife moves to 15 Wielandstrasse.
Charlotte's life is turned upside down.
The apartment, long used to emptiness and silence, is transformed.
Paula brings the cultural life of Berlin into their home.
She invites celebrities.
They meet the famous Albert Einstein.
The architect Erich Mendelsohn.
The theologian Albert Schweitzer.
This is the zenith of German domination.
Intellectual, artistic and scientific.
They play the piano, they drink, they sing, they dance, they invent.
Life has never seemed so intense.

There are now little brass plaques on the ground outside this address.
These are *Stolpersteine*.
Tributes to the victims of the Holocaust.
There are many of them in Berlin, especially in Charlottenburg.
They are not easy to spot.
You must walk with your head down, seeking memories between the
    cobblestones.

In front of 15 Wielandstrasse, three names can be read.
Paula, Albert and Charlotte.
But on the wall, there is only one commemorative plaque.
The one for Charlotte Salomon.

During my last visit to Berlin, it had vanished.
The building was being renovated, under scaffolding.
Charlotte erased for a fresh coat of paint.
Sanitized, the house façade looks like a movie backdrop.
Immobile on the sidewalk, I stare at the balcony.
Where Charlotte posed for a photograph with her father.
The picture was taken around 1928.
She is eleven or twelve, and the look in her eyes is bright.
She already looks surprisingly like a woman.
I dally for a moment in the past.
Preferring to look at the photograph in my memory rather than the present.
Then, finally, I make a decision.
I weave between the ladders and the workmen and go upstairs.
To the second floor, outside her apartment.

I ring Charlotte's doorbell.

Because of the construction work, the place is empty.
But there is a light on in the apartment.
As if someone's there.
There must be someone there.
And yet I hear no sound.
It's a large apartment, I know.
I ring again.
Still nothing.
While I wait, I read the names listed above the doorbell.

Apparently the Salomons' apartment has been turned into offices.
The company headquarters of *Dasdomainhaus.com*.
A firm that develops websites.

I hear a noise.
Footsteps coming closer.
Someone hesitating, then opening the door.
A worried-looking woman appears.
What do we want?
Christian Kolb, my German translator, is with me.
He takes his time before speaking.
Dot dot dot is always in his mouth.
I ask him to explain why we are here.
French writer . . . Charlotte Salomon . . .
She slams the door in our faces.
I stand there stunned, immobile.
I am only a few feet from Charlotte's room.
It's frustrating, but some things should not be forced.
I have plenty of time.

8

Charlotte is enriched by the discussions she hears.
She starts reading: a lot, and with passion.
Devours Goethe, Hesse, Remarque, Nietzsche, Döblin.
Paula thinks her stepdaughter is too withdrawn.
She never invites friends home.

Charlotte becomes possessive with her stepmother.
During parties, she follows her around like a shadow.

Cannot bear other people to spend too long talking to her.
She wants to give Paula something special for her birthday.
She spends whole days searching for the ideal gift.
Finally, she finds the perfect powder compact.
All her pocket money goes toward it.
She is so pleased with her find.
Her stepmother will love her even more.
The evening of the birthday, Charlotte is on tenterhooks.
Paula opens her present.
She is very happy with it.
But it is one gift among many.
She thanks everyone with equal sweetness.
Charlotte falls to pieces.
She is crushed by the disappointment.
Driven crazy.
She rushes over to grab back the compact.
And hurls it on the floor, in front of all the guests.
Silence descends.
Albert looks at Paula, as if it is up to her to react.
The singer is coldly furious.
She accompanies Charlotte to her room.
We'll talk about this tomorrow, she says.
I've ruined everything, thinks Charlotte.

In the morning, they see each other in the kitchen.
Charlotte starts babbling excuses.
She tries to explain what she was feeling.
Paula strokes her cheek, to comfort her.
Glad that Charlotte is finally able to put words to her malaise.
Paula remembers the joyful adolescent she met.
She doesn't understand what it is that troubles her so much now.

For Albert, his daughter's reaction is a manifestation of jealousy.
Nothing more.
He refuses to see the depth of her suffering.
His work takes up all his attention; he is an important doctor.
He is making major discoveries in the treatment of ulcers.
His daughter's tantrums are not his priority.
Paula continues to worry.
She thinks Charlotte should be told everything.
The truth.
What truth? Albert asks.
The truth . . . about her mother.
She insists.
No one can build their identity on such a lie.
If she finds out that everyone has lied to her, it will be awful.
No, Albert replies, we must say nothing about it.
Then adds: her grandparents are adamant.
They do not want her to know.

Paula suddenly understands.
Charlotte often goes to stay at their house.
The pressure is incessant.
They never let anyone forget that they have lost their daughters.
Lotte is all that's left to them, they moan.
When she returns from staying with them, Charlotte is somber.
Her grandmother loves her very deeply, of course.
But there is a dark power to her love.
How can that woman look after a child?
That woman whose two daughters killed themselves.

9

Paula agrees not to reveal anything to Charlotte.
As that is the family's wish.
But she sends a scathing letter to the grandmother.
"You are the murderer of your daughters.
But this time you won't have her.
I am going to protect her . . ."
Devastated, the grandmother withdraws into herself.
The past she attempted to bury is coming back in waves.
She lets the successive tragedies overwhelm her.

There are her two daughters, of course.
But they are only the culmination of a long line of suicides.
Her brother too threw himself in a river, because of an unhappy marriage.
A doctor of law, he was only twenty-eight.
His corpse was exhibited in the living room.
For days on end, the family slept close to the tragedy.
They didn't want to let him leave.
The apartment would be his tomb.
Only the stink of decomposition put an end to the exhibition.
When they came to pick up her son, the mother tried to stop them.
She could accept his death, not his absence.
Not the absence of his body.
She sank into insanity.
Two full-time nurses were hired.
To protect her from herself.
As would later happen to Franziska, just after her first suicide attempt.

So history would repeat itself.
Repeat itself endlessly, like the refrain of the dead.

The grandmother remembers such difficult years.
When she had to constantly watch her own mother.
She would speak to her sometimes to soothe her.
This seemed to calm her down.
But inevitably she started mentioning her son again.
She said he was a sailor.
That was why they didn't see much of him.
And then suddenly the reality would hit her in the face.
It would bite, hard.
And she would scream for hours.
After eight years of mental exhaustion, she finally succumbed.
Perhaps the family would be able to find a semblance of peace.

But it wasn't over for Charlotte's grandmother.
No sooner was their mother in the ground than her younger sister
    committed suicide.
Inexplicably, unforeseeably.
At eighteen years old, she got up in the night.
And threw herself in the icy river.
Just as the first Charlotte would do later.
So history would repeat itself.
Repeat itself endlessly, like the refrain of the dead.

The grandmother had been paralyzed by her sister's death.
She had not seen it coming—and nor had anyone else.
She had to get away, fast.
Marriage was the best option.
She became a Grunwald.
And quickly had two daughters.

44

. . .

A few years passed, strangely happy.
But the black march began again.
Her brother's only daughter committed suicide.
And then it was her father's turn, and then her aunt's.
So there would never be any escape.
The morbid atavism was too powerful.
The roots of a family tree gnawed at by evil.

And yet she never would have thought her own daughters contaminated.
Nothing suggested it during their happy childhood.
They ran all over the place.
Jumped, danced, laughed.
It was unthinkable.
Charlotte, then Franziska.

Shut away in her room, the grandmother continues to mourn her dead.
The letter lying on her lap.
Soaked with tears, the words blur, distort.
What if Paula was right?
After all, that woman sings like an angel.
Yes, what she says is true.
Everyone around her dies.
So she must be careful.
Protect Charlotte.
She will see her less often, if it's better that way.
Her granddaughter will no longer come to stay here.
That is the essential thing.
Charlotte must live.
But is that even possible?

Part Three

Charlotte is now sixteen.
A serious girl, brilliant at school.
People sometimes find her mysterious.
Her stepmother considers her insolent, above all.
They no longer get along so well.
Albert is still obsessed with his medical explorations.
So the two of them spend long days together.
Getting on each other's nerves, growing irritable: what could be more
    normal?
Charlotte is increasingly divided.
She idolizes Paula, and she can't bear her.

But she never tires of hearing her sing.
She goes to all her concerts in Berlin.
And feels the same emotion she felt the first time.
Paula is one of the greatest living divas.
Crowds rush to hear her.
One night, she records a magnificent version of *Carmen*.
Charlotte is in the first row that night.
Her stepmother holds the note a long time.
The last note of the concert.
The audience holds its breath.
The sound fades elegantly.
It's a triumph, an ovation, something even greater if that's possible.
Here and there, people shout bravos.

Charlotte observes the bouquets of flowers that clutter the stage.
The bouquets that will soon decorate their living room.
Everything is red.
And in the heart of this redness, a dissonant note.

To begin with, Charlotte is not sure.
Perhaps it's a slightly strange form of admiration.
The shouting grows more raucous, the whistling more shrill.
No, it's not admiration.
It's coming from somewhere above.
It's still not easy to see.
The lights have not come back on yet.
The noise grows louder.
Now the boos are drowning out the applause.
Paula understands, and runs backstage.
She does not want to listen to that.
She does not want to hear their hatred.

Men yell insults, horrible things.
They tell Paula to go home.
They don't want to hear her anymore here!
Charlotte, trembling, goes to find her.
She expects to find her stepmother devastated.
But no, there she is, standing in front of her mirror.
She looks strong, almost unshakeable.
It is she who reassures Charlotte.
We have to get used to it, that's just how it is . . .
But her voice rings false.
Her veneer of calm cannot hide her anxiety.

Back at home, Albert is still not asleep.
He is aghast when he hears what happened.

The scene they describe makes him want to throw up.
It is becoming simply unbearable.
Some of their friends are going to leave Germany.
These friends encourage them to do the same.
Paula could sing in the United States.
Albert could easily find work there.
No, he says.
It's out of the question.
This is their homeland.
This is Germany.
They must be optimistic,[1] must believe that the hatred is ephemeral.

2

In January 1933, the hatred comes to power.

Paula no longer has the right to perform in public.
For Albert, professional death will surely follow too.
Medical care carried out by Jews is no longer reimbursed.
He imagines them taking away his teaching diploma.
He who has made important discoveries.
Attacks are spreading, books are burning.
In the Salomons' apartment, they meet up in the evenings.
Artists, intellectuals, doctors.
Some continue to believe this is a passing phase.
The logical consequences of an economic crisis.
Someone must always be blamed for a nation's woes.
Charlotte listens to the discussions of the destroyed.

[1] Billy Wilder said: "The optimists died in the gas chambers; the pessimists have pools in Beverly Hills."

Kurt Singer is there too.
He has just lost his job at the Berlin Opera.
His strength and charisma drive him to lead the resistance.
He makes approaches to the Nazis.
He pleads the causes of dismissed artists.
Proposes the creation of a cultural federation of German Jews.
Hearing this, the party leader hesitates.
He ought to refuse, but he can't help admiring Singer.
For a moment, time stands still between them.
In that moment, anything might happen.
The artists' definitive death, or their survival.
The bureaucrat has the power to ban everything.
For now, he says nothing.
He looks into Singer's eyes.
Singer holds back the sweat that ought to bead his forehead.
Each man's future is in the balance.

After several long minutes, the Nazi official takes out a sheet of paper.
He signs the authorization to create a Jewish association.
Singer thanks him effusively.
Thank you, sir, thank you so much.
All hail the artists' hero.
A big party is organized to celebrate this victory.
What joy: they are not going to die immediately.
Singers, actors, dancers, professors all breathe.
To be onstage is to be alive.
Paula will not be reduced to silence.
She can still give concerts.
In a Jewish theater, for a Jewish audience.
The cultural version of the ghetto.
This system will last a few years.

The restrictions gradually becoming tighter, more rigorous, more
    suffocating.

In 1938, Kurt Singer leaves to visit his sister in the United States.
During his absence, *Kristallnacht* happens.
Jewish goods are pillaged, dozens of people murdered.
Kurt's sister begs him to stay in America.
It's an incredible stroke of luck for him.
He can be spared from the coming disaster.
He is even offered a position at the university.
But no.
He is determined to return to his homeland.
To save what can be saved, he says.

On his return to Europe, he travels through Rotterdam.
There too, his friends try to convince him to stay.
The cultural association has been dissolved in any case.
Going back to Germany in 1938 would be suicide.
He yields, and settles down in Holland.
Once again, he attempts to resist through music and art.
He gives concerts.
But even there, the noose is tightening.
So many times, he could have fled.
But he wanted to be close to his loved ones.
An illusory shield for the fragility of others.
He is such a brave man.
The photographs show his power, his crazy hair.
He will be deported in 1942, to the Terezin concentration camp.
Where, among others, the artists and the elite are held.
It's a so-called model camp.
A showcase for the Red Cross delegations.

Those visitors, blind to what is hidden behind the scenery.
Plays are put on for them, a sign that all is well.
Singer even continues organizing concerts.
He lifts his arm, conducts the orchestra with his baton.
What remains of the orchestra.
Month after month, the musicians sink into silence.
And die without ceremony.
Singer ends up helping two sickly violinists.
He continues till the end, urging the dying to stay alive.
Nobody believes anymore, nobody but him.
Until the day when he collapses with exhaustion, in January 1944.
Killed in action.

3

But let us return to 1933.

Charlotte no longer believes that the hatred might be a passing phase.
It is not coming from a few fanatics, but an entire nation.
The country is led by a pack of bloodthirsty hounds.
In early April, a boycott of Jewish goods is organized.
She watches protesters parade through the streets, sees shops being pillaged.
Anyone who buys from a Jew is a swine, she reads.
Angry crowds chant slogans.
Can we imagine Charlotte's terror?
Humiliating new laws are constantly announced.
At school, students must provide their grandparents' birth certificates.
Some girls have Jewish ancestors, it turns out.
One second they are German, the next they are banished.
The fear of bad blood.

Some mothers forbid their daughters to hang around with Jewish girls.
What if it's contagious?
Others are outraged.
They must come together and fight the Nazis, they protest.
But such talk is dangerous.
So people speak out ever more quietly.
Until finally they fall silent for good.

Albert does his best to reassure his daughter.
But do any words have the power to diminish other people's hatred?
Charlotte withdraws further into herself.
She reads constantly, dreams less and less.
It is during this period that drawing enters her life.
Her passion for the Renaissance enables her to leave behind her own era.

4

Charlotte's grandparents often go away in the summer.
This year, they are taking a long cultural trip around Italy.
And they want to take their granddaughter.
Despite the anxieties of the past, her father and Paula don't hesitate.
She will be happy far from the abyss.

For Charlotte, this trip will prove crucial.
Her grandparents are crazy about ancient civilizations.
About anything that resembles a ruin.
They are especially fascinated by mummies.
And by painting, of course.
Charlotte deepens her knowledge.
Discovers new horizons.

In front of certain pictures, her heart pounds as if she was in love.
Summer 1933: the true birth date of her destiny.

A precise point exists in the trajectory of any artist.
The moment where his or her voice begins to be heard.
Density spreads through it, like blood through water.

During the journey, Charlotte asks questions about her mother.
The memory of her presence has faded through the years.
It's been reduced to vague sensations, imprecise emotions.
It hurts to have forgotten her voice, her scent.
The grandmother avoids the subject: too painful.
Charlotte realizes it is better not to ask anything.
Franziska continues her journey in silence.
The cause of her death remains secret to her daughter.

The grandfather comforts himself with works of art.
They give him an absurd optimism.
Europe will not sink into murderous insanity again.
This is what he declares when they visit the ruins.
The power of ancient civilizations is reassuring.
As he spouts his theories, his arms wave wildly.
His wife follows him, her husband's eternal shadow.
Watching this improbable duo, Charlotte smiles.
They look so old.
The grandfather sports a long white beard, like an apostle.
He walks with a stick, though he remains robust.
The grandmother is increasingly skeletal.
Kept on her feet by a miraculous secret known only to her.

The two old people stride relentlessly through galleries.
Charlotte is the one who keeps begging for a break.

She's exhausted by the insistent pace.
All three of them want to see every museum.
Charlotte thinks sometimes that this constant craving is futile.
Wouldn't it be better to grow attached to a single work?
To offer it her exclusive gaze?
Surely it is preferable to know one picture perfectly.
Rather than squander her attention and finally lose it.
She wants so much to settle on something.
To stop searching for what she cannot find.

5

The return to Germany is difficult.
After a summer surrounded by wonders, reality is an attack.
This reality that they must look in the face.
So the grandparents decide to leave their country.
They do not expect ever to go back.
Their exile will be definitive.

They met an American once, during a trip to Spain.
Of German origin, Ottilie Moore is recently widowed.
So it is that she finds herself heir to a fortune.
She owns a vast estate in the South of France.
Where she welcomes all kinds of refugees, children especially.
While visiting Berlin, she becomes aware of the violence.
She offers to let the grandparents stay with her.
For an unlimited time, she adds.
She appreciates their erudition and their humor.
With her, they would be sheltered from the coming storm.
After a long hesitation, they agree.

In Villefranche-sur-Mer, the property is a little piece of paradise.
With gardens that are beautiful, even exotic.
Filled with olive trees, palms, cypresses.
Ottilie is a cheerful woman, always smiling, almost exuberant.

Charlotte stays in Berlin with her father and Paula.
She goes back to school, where the humiliations never end.
Until the day when a law forbids her from pursuing her studies.
One year before her *baccalauréat* exam, she has to drop out.
She leaves with a school report praising her *impeccable behavior*.

She and Paula live like hermits in the apartment.
Not only do they not support each other, they don't even understand each
    other anymore.
Charlotte blames her stepmother for her exclusion from the world.
Paula is the only person she can yell at.

Some days are calmer.
They talk about the future.
Charlotte draws more and more, dreams of joining the art school in Berlin.
Sometimes she walks to the building and stands out in front.
She watches the students come out carrying their portfolios.
Then she lifts her eyes.
A huge Nazi flag flies from a pole on the roof.

Her father tells her it will be complicated to join the Academy.
They accept only a very small quota of Jews, barely 1 percent.
He encourages her to enroll in a fashion design school instead.
There, Semites are tolerated.
And it will still be artistic.
She could create clothes.

Reluctantly, she agrees.
After all, she has given up deciding how to live her life.
Stupefied, she stays there only one day.
But those few hours make her sure of her vocation.
She wants to paint.

Her first pictures are promising, it's true.
Albert decides to pay for private lessons.
It's essential she receive a proper training, he says.
Yes, it's essential for the future.

6

The lessons turn out to be pitiful.
Her professor seems to think that painting ended in 1650.
This woman bundled up in an old-fashioned beige suit.
With her Coke-bottle glasses, she looks like a frog.
Charlotte tries to comply obediently.
After all, this is a financial sacrifice for her father.
But the boredom is immeasurable.
The frog asks her to draw a cactus.
Several times, she coldly erases Charlotte's drawing.
The number of thorns is not correct!
This isn't painting, it's photography.
For weeks on end, Charlotte does nothing but still lifes.
This seems apt, as her own life is so still, so silent.
Charlotte cannot express what she feels.
Her drawing improves, though.
She finds a style midway between the traditional and the modern.
She deeply admires Van Gogh, discovers Chagall.

She reveres Emil Nolde, who once said:
"I like it when a picture looks as if it painted itself."
There's Munch too, of course, and Kokoschka and Beckmann.
Nothing but painting matters now: it has become an obsession.
She absolutely has to apply to the art school in Berlin.
She prepares rigorously.
The demon grows inside her.
Albert and Paula begin to worry about the intensity of her passion.
But for Charlotte it is a source of joy.
After feeling so lost, she has at last found her way.

She presents her portfolio to the art school.
Professor Ludwig Bartning is intrigued by her style.
He senses an immense potential in this candidate.
He is adamant she must join the Academy.
But so few Jews are admitted.
The only point in her favor: Charlotte's father is a military veteran.
Occasionally one can find breathing spaces in the general suffocation.
But nothing is certain yet.
First they must present her portfolio to the committee.
Ludwig wants to meet the young artist.
He is a kindly man, who campaigns against the racial laws.
Charlotte will become his protégée.
Perhaps he sees something in her that he does not possess?
Ludwig paints flowers.
Elegant flowers.
But perfectly calm and rational flowers.
The day of the admission committee, the tension is palpable.
Charlotte's talent is obvious.
But it is out of the question that she should join the art school.
It's too much of a risk.

Where is the risk? Bartning demands indignantly.
She could pose a danger to the young Aryans.
Jewish girls are temptresses, deviants.
Bartning says he has met Charlotte.

He guarantees that she does not represent any kind of threat to the
    students.
And he goes further: she is actually very shy.
In this way the potential menace of Charlotte is analyzed.
Her talent is not even mentioned.
In the end, though, Ludwig Bartning's insistence is rewarded.
It is a remarkable victory.
Charlotte Salomon, excluded everywhere else, is admitted.
She will study at the Academy of Fine Arts in Berlin.

7

Thrilled and eager, she gets down to work.
Her professors appreciate her rigor, her inventiveness.
Sometimes they reproach her for being so silent.
They need to figure out what they want.
She has been told to act discreetly, not to speak to other students.
She does manage to make a friend, however.
Barbara, the beautiful blonde, the quintessential Aryan girl.
I'm so beautiful, heil Hitler! says Barbara.
They like to walk home together in the evenings.
Charlotte listens as her friend confides in her.
She tells her about her beaux.
Her life seems wonderful.
If only Charlotte could be a little bit Barbara.

· · ·

At the Academy, artistic freedom is gradually reined in.
The professors are subject to stricter constraints.
The Nazis have decided to bring the painters to heel.
Armed men sometimes storm into the building.
And stand there, inhaling the scent of decadence.
Modern art must quite simply be eradicated.
How dare anyone paint anything other than blond peasants?
Athletes must be glorified, strength and virility honored.
Certainly not the twisted, torn, mad-eyed figures of Beckmann's pictures.
How horrific that artist is, the very essence of degenerate art.

Beckmann, a German genius, decides to leave his country in 1937,
After hearing Hitler's speech in Munich.
The speech he gave at the opening of the German House of Art:
"Before National Socialism took power . . .
There existed in Germany so-called modern art.
Every year a new modern art!
What we want is a German art with eternal values!
Art is not founded on time, an era, a style, a year.
But solely on a people!
And what do you produce?
Twisted cripples and cretins.
Women who can inspire only disgust.
Men who look more like animals than human beings.
Children who, if they existed in real life . . .
Would be immediately considered a divine curse!"
Thus defined, degenerate art is at the heart of a major retrospective.
To show what people are forbidden to like.
The eye must be educated, an army of taste molded.
And above all: those guilty of decadence must be named and shamed.

Place of honor is given to Marc Chagall, Max Ernst and Otto Dix.
They come in droves to vomit on artistic Jewishness.
First they burned books, now they spit on paintings.
Alongside the works of art, there are exhibitions of children's scribblings.
Or pictures painted by mentally handicapped people.
So the stage is set for the execution of modern art.

8

Charlotte positions herself on the side of the despised artists.
She is interested in pictorial progress, in the latest theories.
She owns books by the art historian Aby Warburg.
When I discovered this, it all seemed clear to me.

Before I knew about Charlotte, I was fascinated by Aby Warburg.
In 1998, I read an article in *Libération*.
The title was: "Rescuing Warburg."
The journalist Robert Maggiori mentioned a *mythical library*.
The word library stopped me in my tracks.
I am looking for one, which has haunted me as long as I remember.
It is a childhood vision, an obsession.
Is it a memory of a previous life?

Something drew me to that name: Aby Warburg.
So I read everything I could find about that strange character.
Heir to a fortune, the firstborn, he bequeaths all his money to his
   brothers.
On the sole condition that they will buy him any book he asks for.
So Aby Warburg is able to create an unprecedented collection.
He has his own theories on how books should be arranged.

Most famously the "good neighbor" theory.
The book we are looking for is not necessarily the one we should read.
We should look at the one next to it.

He walks among his books for hours, in ecstasy.
On the edge of insanity, he also talks to butterflies.
He will be institutionalized on numerous occasions.
So he summons all the doctors.
And attempts to prove to them that he is not crazy.
If I prove it, you must set me free!
After his death, in 1929, his work endures thanks to his disciples.
Foremost among them is Ernst Cassirer.
Sensing the coming danger, he decides to save the library.
He transfers it to London in 1933 (books fleeing Nazism).
It is still there now, in Woburn Square.
I have often been to visit.

In July 2004, I received a grant for a literary journey.
The name of the grant is a *Mission Stendhal*.
I had to go to Hamburg, to visit the house where Warburg was born.
I wanted to write a book about him, of course.
But I also wanted to bring my infatuation into contact with reality.
Because I couldn't stop thinking about him.
His personality, his epoch, the story of the exiled library.
I went, certain I would find illumination.
But nothing happened.
What exactly did I expect?
I no longer even knew what I had gone to look for.
Increasingly, I felt myself attracted to Germany.
And obsessed by the language.
I listened to *lieder* sung by Kathleen Ferrier.

In several of my novels, my characters speak German.
Certain heroines teach or translate that language.
I navigated my way by this vague intuition.
All the artists I loved were Germanic.
Even the designers, which is saying something.
Nothing interests me less than furniture.
But I adored Bauhaus-era desks.
I went to the Conran Shop just to look at them.
I would open drawers the way others try on shoes.
And there was Berlin: I was falling in love with Berlin.
I would spend hours on the terrace of a café in Savignyplatz.
Or leafing through art books in the area's bookstores.
Apparently my infatuation was fashionable.
It's true, everyone loves Berlin.
I am surrounded by people who want to live there.
But I didn't feel fashionable.
On the contrary, I was old and passé.

And then I discovered Charlotte's work.
Purely by chance.
I had no idea what I was going to see.
I was eating lunch with a friend who worked in a museum.
She told me: you have to see this exhibition.
That's all she said.
Maybe she added: I think you'll like it.
But I'm not sure.
There was nothing premeditated about it.
She led me to the exhibition room.
And it was instant.
The feeling of having finally found what I was looking for.
The unexpected climax to all my vague longings.

My wanderings had brought me to the right place.
I knew it as soon as I discovered *Life? or Theater?*
Everything I loved.
Everything that had infatuated me for years.
Warburg and painting.
German writers.
Music and fantasy.
Despair and madness.
It was all there.
In a blaze of bright colors.

The immediate complicity with someone.
The strange sensation of having already come to a place.
I had all of that with Charlotte's work.
I already knew what I was discovering.

The friend, who was standing close to me, asked: so, do you like it?
I couldn't answer her.
Too much emotion.
She must have thought I wasn't interested.
Whereas in fact . . .
I don't know.
I didn't know how to express what I was feeling.

Not long ago, I came upon a short essay by Jonathan Safran Foer.
He is not an author whose work I really know.
But I feel a slightly idiotic sympathy for him.
Because the two of us are sometimes placed next to each other on
    bookstore shelves.
We create connections the best we can.
Another version of the good neighbor theory.

In the essay, he describes the shock he felt when he discovered Charlotte.
It was in Amsterdam.
He too found her by chance.
He mentions the important meeting he had that day.
Which literally escaped his memory.
I emerged in the same state of mind.
Nothing else mattered.
It is so rare, that feeling of being completely overwhelmed.
I was an occupied country.
Days passed, and nothing happened to alter that sensation.

For years, I took notes.
I pored over her work incessantly.
I quoted or mentioned Charlotte in several of my novels.
I tried to write this book so many times.
But how?
Should I be present?
Should I fictionalize her story?
What form should my obsession take?
I began, I tried, then I gave up.
I couldn't manage to string two sentences together.
At every point, I felt blocked.
Impossible to go on.
It was a physical sensation, an oppression.
I felt the need to move to the next line in order to breathe.

So, I realized that I had to write it like this.

Part Four

1

An important event in Charlotte's life occurs now.
This event is a man.

It is impossible to say whether Alfred Wolfsohn is handsome or ugly.
Some appearances are like an unanswerable question.
You simply know that you can't look away.
When he is there, he is all you see.

At the moment when I am searching for him in order to describe him,
    he is walking fast.
Striding through the streets of Berlin, covered in sweat.
He has to take care of his sick mother, of his unemployable sister.
But where can he earn money?
A singing teacher, he is no longer allowed to do his job anywhere.
All that remains to him is the *Kulturbund*.
The mutual aid association founded by Kurt Singer.
He is the only person that can help Alfred.

Late as always, he finally enters Singer's office.
He stammers a few incomprehensible excuses.
Arms whirling excitedly.
Despite the comic effect of this appearance, Singer doesn't smile.
Because Alfred is an eminent man.
He is strange and capricious, but hugely talented.
He has developed new theories on singing methods.
You must search for your voice deep inside yourself.

How is it possible for babies to scream for so long?
Without even damaging their vocal cords.
You must return to the source of this power.
A crazy dive down to what is hidden within us.
And all of this has perhaps some connection with death.

Alfred is charming: people want to help him, to save him even.
Kurt thinks about it, then glimpses a solution.
The great opera singer Paula Salomon no longer has a teacher.
The one who worked with her for so long has just quit.
Reluctantly, he put an end to their collaboration.
He had no choice.
He was in danger if he continued working with a Jew.
Their final lesson was intensely painful.
They separated on the landing, in silence.

A few days later, the doorbell rings.
It must be the teacher sent by Kurt Singer.
That's good: he's on time for a change.
She opens the door, shows him in.
Before even taking off his coat, he says: this is an honor.
Before even saying hello, in fact.
A compliment that makes Paula happy.
Praise is increasingly rare these days.
She hardly ever sings in public anymore.
They have taken away her right to be applauded.
But she must continue to work on her voice.
Because she will be back one day, undoubtedly.

Alfred walks straight over to the piano.
Ahead of Paula, as if he's at home.

He strokes the instrument, and only then does he take off his coat.
He turns toward his hostess, and looks her in the eyes.
After a moment of silence, he launches into a monologue.
You must hire me, it's essential.
You sang better before, at the start of your career.
The routine of success has deadened you.
Your last record was horribly mechanical.
I can tell you honestly: it has no soul.
You have an immense talent, but that is not enough.
I will make you the greatest opera singer in the world.
My methods are revolutionary, you'll see.
Or rather, you'll hear.

He talks on and on, as Paula stands dumbstruck.
How dare he?
How can he show up and pontificate so presumptuously?
And yet, he's not completely wrong.
Paula senses that her relationship with music has become too unemotional.
What happened?
Is it because of the political situation?
Or has success numbed everything?
This man was supposed to help her, but now she feels lost.
No one has delivered so many harsh truths to her in a long, long time.

Alfred is taking a considerable risk.
He desperately needs a job.
It is an act of hubris, speaking to her like this.
She could send him packing.
Who is he to judge her in this way?
He continues speaking as he paces the living room.
Hands behind his back.

Will he ever stop?
Paula wants to interrupt him, to say: I understand.
She wants to, but it's impossible.
Whole centuries of words seem to pour from Alfred's mouth.
He has not even been entrusted with this task yet, and already he has taken it to heart.
Paula realizes she should not dig her heels in.
This man, however clumsy, has good intentions.
He wants nothing more than to teach her his beliefs.

She lifts her hand to signal that he should finally be quiet.
It does no good: he talks and talks.
Paula does not grasp everything he says.
Apparently he's in the middle of an anecdote about Bach.
At last, he sees her hand in the air.
And, suddenly, he stops.
Paula feels exhausted by what she has heard.
But she finds enough strength to say: you start tomorrow morning.
I'll expect you here at ten.

2

This is the beginning of an intense relationship.
Each morning, they come together at the piano.
While this is happening, Albert heals the sick.
And Charlotte draws herself.
At the Academy, she is studying self-portraiture.

Alfred is now a real diversion for Paula.
He is charming, eccentric, incredibly erudite.

He talks for hours.
Her teacher is obsessed by the myth of Orpheus.
In fact, he's writing a book on the subject.
He thinks constantly about crossing through darkness.
How does one recover from a state of chaos?
To understand his obsession, we must go back into the past.

At barely eighteen, he leaves for the front.
He wants to run away, disappear, but it's impossible.
A man's life then is a soldier's life.
And so he faces up to the worst.
He knows fear.
Standing in the mist, forbidden to retrace his steps.
All deserters will be shot.
The clouds are so low.
The churned earth stinks of decomposed bodies.
The landscape is one vast desolation.
Like Otto Dix, Alfred thinks this is *the devil's work*.

An attack decimates his regiment.
All around him, he sees mutilated bodies.
Surely he is dead too.
And yet, something continues to beat inside him.
It must be his heart, hidden in the depths of his body.
His ears hurt.
The explosion perforated his eardrums.
All the same, he thinks he can hear someone calling.
Or are they groaning?
Alfred opens his eyes, so he must be alive.
He sees the soldier dying next to him.
Begging for help.

In this instant, Alfred perceives a presence.
French soldiers moving toward them.
Probably searching for survivors to finish off.
He can't help the other soldier.
He can't.
It's not possible.
He must leave him like that.
To a certain death.
Alfred crawls under a corpse.
And stops breathing.

How long does he stay like that?
Impossible to say.
Finally, a patrol picks up the wounded.
Alfred remembers nothing more.
Sent back to Berlin, he does not even recognize his mother.
He remains like this for a year.
For him, 1919 does not exist.
He can't speak anymore, is sent to sanatoriums.
With other broken men.
Months pass, and he has to leave that hell behind him.
And, above all, never turn back, like Orpheus.

In the heart of darkness, a melody sounds.
To begin with, it is barely audible.
It is the rebirth of his voice.
He starts to sing, very softly.
More than ever, music and life are intertwined.
That is why Alfred throws himself into song: to survive.
The way you might throw yourself into water in order to die.

3

In Alfred's hands, Paula senses she is making progress.
She lets herself be guided entirely by him.
Sometimes he is cruel to her.
He will cut her off in the middle of a lied.
And yell at her for having the wrong tempo.
She bursts out laughing when that happens.
He takes his work so seriously.
How can we describe the way he feels?
Let's just say he feels he is where he belongs.
Something keeps him here.
In truth, he has fallen in love.
He writes a few impassioned letters to Paula.
Oh, come now, be serious.
You love being with me, but you don't love me.
Maybe she is right.
Alfred is simply happy to feel his heart beating.

That day, Charlotte comes home earlier than expected.
She wants to meet the famous singing teacher.
Master and student do not hear her.
Paula makes strange cries, as Alfred grows overexcited.
He lifts his arms, as if to touch the ceiling.
Charlotte can't believe it.
Again, again, again! Alfred demands.
Her cry is so piercing, it is almost inaudible.
Charlotte puts her hands to her ears.
She doesn't dare show herself, or warn them of her presence.

But Paula suddenly spots her, and the cry ceases.

Ah, it's my Lotte.

Come in here, darling, come closer.

Let me introduce you to Herr Wolfsohn.

No need for that, she can call me Alfred.

Charlotte walks over slowly.

So slowly, it's as if she's not moving at all.

4

When the lesson is over, Alfred goes into Charlotte's room.

She is drawing at her desk, but she freezes when she sees her visitor.

He observes the room in great detail.

So, you're studying at the Academy?

Yes.

Yes: that is the first word she speaks to this man.

Alfred starts asking lots of questions.

Which painters does she like best?

Does she have a favorite color?

Does she like the Renaissance?

Does she support the degenerate artists?

How often does she go to the movie theater?

He speaks too quickly, the words cascading from his mouth.

Charlotte, lost, mixes up her answers.

She says "mauve" when he asks her if she's seen *Metropolis*.

Paula enters the room.

My dear Wolfsohn, leave this child in peace.

I love her like my own daughter, so please don't annoy her.

He's not bothering me, Charlotte replies.
It is rare to see her react this way.
Usually, she hesitates.
Eons pass between her thoughts and her words.
Paula is surprised.
Is she jealous?
No, she's not in love with Alfred.
On the contrary, she is glad that he's interested in Charlotte.
Her stepdaughter meets so few people.
She is cloistered in her drawings, almost like a nun.
So Paula vacates the room, leaving them alone.

Alfred examines Charlotte's sketches.
She is overwhelmed by fear.
Her body trembles, on the inside.
You have an above-average talent.
Damned with faint praise?
No, Charlotte is encouraged.
This man is in her room, and he is attentive.
A drawing catches his eye.
What have you represented here?
It's inspired by a Matthias Claudius poem.
Well, it's in the Schubert libretto.
I illustrated *Death and the Maiden*.
Alfred looks troubled.
Then says simply: death and the maiden, that's us.

Charlotte softly speaks the words of the Maiden:

Pass me by! Oh, pass me by!
Go, fierce man of bones!

I am still young. Go, rather.
And do not touch me.

And Alfred responds with Death's words:

Give me your hand, you beautiful and tender form!
I am a friend, and come not to punish.
Be of good cheer! I am not fierce.
Softly shall you sleep in my arms.

For a moment, they remain in silence.
Then, without a word, Alfred leaves the room.
Charlotte gets up and stands close to the window.
One minute later, she sees the professor in the street.
Will he turn around to look at her?
No, what a ridiculous idea.
He has already forgotten her.
He just came in to say hello.
A question of politeness.
And what about the way he looked at her drawings?
Common courtesy, nothing more.
He did seem sincere, though.
She doesn't know, she doesn't know anything anymore.

From her window, she watches him walk away down the street.
He does not turn around, becomes smaller and smaller.
She tries to follow his progress as long as possible.
As he walks, he moves his head.
As if he were talking to himself.

5

Coming out of the Academy, Charlotte too walks quickly.
Barbara tries to hold her back, but it's no good.
She is left alone, and this makes her sad.
Charlotte is usually such a good listener.
Her ears are perfect recipients for Barbara's secrets.
She tells her friend everything, even the kiss she shared with Klaus.
But now she feels a strange emotion.
However dull Charlotte's life may appear, Barbara sometimes envies her.
There is something powerful and touching about her.
Is it the charisma of the silent?
Or the sad strength radiated by those excluded from society?
Barbara has everything, except what Charlotte has.
So she runs after her.
But Charlotte is already far away.

She tries to see Alfred whenever she can.
If she gets home too late, she collapses on her bed.
Ever since he entered her room, she has felt under his power.
Under the power of his gaze.
She paints for him, to win his approval.
She feels idiotic.
She has seen him several times since that first meeting.
He has given her nothing more than a quick smile.
Never taking the time to ask about her again.
Did his interest in her last only a single day?
Perhaps there is some logic to all this.
If an entire country can reject you, what hope can you have with a man?

Just when she has stopped believing it will happen, Alfred reappears.

He comes into her room without knocking.

She looks up.

I hope I'm not disturbing you?

No, no, I was just daydreaming.

I have a proposal to make to you, he goes on.

His tone is serious, almost authoritarian.

Charlotte's eyes grow wide.

It's . . . delicate, he begins.

I've written something . . . something very personal.

Yes, this book is about me.

I believe any work of art should reveal its author.

I mean, I have nothing against fiction.

But all that stuff is just entertainment.

And people need to be entertained.

It's their way of not seeing the truth.

Anyway, it's not important, that's my point.

We know the meaning of disorder.

And nothing is more important than that, you understand?

It is up to us to decide the perfect moment for chaos.

And it is up to us to decide the moment of death, of course.

I still possess the freedom to do something crazy.

And so do you, don't you?

I know you won't disappoint me.

I have great hopes for you.

Alfred pauses for an instant.

Anything he asks, Charlotte will do.

His presence alone makes every moment intense.

I would like you to illustrate my novel, he says finally.

Without even waiting for her answer, he picks up his bag.
And takes out a stack of papers covered in scribbles.
Charlotte carefully takes hold of the manuscript.
She quickly glances over the opening lines.
When she looks up again, he's gone.

6

Charlotte reads Alfred's book several times.
In a notebook, she writes down the key words.
The story describes the time he spent beneath a corpse.
We can leave anything behind except our obsessions.
Many scenes seem to emerge from darkness.
She sees beauty in the expression of fear.
Isn't she herself in a state of constant dread?
When she walks, speaks, breathes.
She is not allowed in parks or swimming pools.
Her entire city is a battlefield.
A prison for her blood.

She begins with sketches.
For hours, days, nights.
Her entire life is between parentheses.
She wants so badly to live up to his trust.
He arranges to meet her.
In two weeks' time, at the café near the train station.
That way, they will see each other without Paula knowing.

On the day in question, she puts on some lipstick.
Will he make fun of her?

Of her desire to be feminine?
In the end, she wipes it off her lips.
Then reapplies it.
She doesn't know what she should do.
To make a man find her beautiful.
No one ever looks at her.
Either that, or she is the one who never notices anything.
Barbara has told her that Klaus thinks she's pretty.
Well, no, pretty is not the word he used.
He said that her face is full of strength.
What does that mean?
For Klaus, it's a compliment.
He thinks Barbara is pretty, but characterless.
But Charlotte couldn't care less about Klaus.
What she wants is for Alfred to like her.

She waits for him in the café, near the central station.
By arranging to meet here, they are breaking the law.
Sitting at a table, she stares at the big clock.
Alfred is late.
Has he forgotten?
Does she have the wrong day?
It's impossible that he won't come.
Finally he arrives, thirty minutes after the agreed time.
And walks quickly over toward Charlotte.
He didn't even have to look for her.
As if he knew instinctively where she was.
By the time he sits down, he is already speaking.
Maybe he began his sentence a while ago.
He lifts his hand to order a beer.
Charlotte is stunned by his appearance.

He turns his head left and right.
As if attracted by everything that is not her.

The waiter brings his beer, and he drinks it right away.
Down in one, not even breathing between mouthfuls.
Only then does he apologize for being late.
Charlotte says it doesn't matter.
But he is not listening to her.
He starts talking about Kafka.
Just like that: a sudden burst of Kafka.
I wanted to tell you, Charlotte, about my revelation.
Kafka's entire oeuvre is based on surprise.
That's his main theme.
If you read his books carefully, you'll see: surprise.
Surprise at his transformation, at being arrested, surprise at himself.
Charlotte does not know how to respond.
She had prepared things to say, analyses.
She was ready to talk about Alfred's novel.
But not about Kafka.
Where Kafka is concerned, she is devoid of words.

Thankfully, he asks to see her drawings.
Charlotte takes out her portfolio, stuffed with sheets.
Alfred is surprised by how much work she has done.
He thinks: this girl must love me.
He might draw some satisfaction from that.
But today, something is suffocating him.
His mood is at rock bottom.
It is simply not the right moment.
He glances quickly at Charlotte's work.
Then says he doesn't have time to give his opinion.

The way he does this is humiliating.
Why is he acting like this?
This man who is usually so gentle and kindly.
He gets up and says he has to go.
He grabs the portfolio as he leaves.
She doesn't even have time to think about getting up too.
He fled so quickly.
It's already over.
You could hardly even call it a meeting.

Charlotte remains behind alone, in a daze.
She stumbles out of the café.
It's so cold now in Berlin.
Where should she go?
She doesn't recognize anything anymore.
Her vision blurs.
Because of the tears in her eyes.
She could throw herself off a bridge.
And die in the icy water.
Her sorrow transforms into morbid urges.
Yes, she must die, as quickly as possible.
Suddenly, a strange feeling overwhelms her.
She has to find out what Alfred thinks of her drawings.
She could be mad at him, but no.
His opinion is still more important than her life.

7

The days pass without any news.
Charlotte doesn't dare ask Paula the date of her next lesson.

She must wait in silence.
In any case, Alfred will return.
Returning is what he does best.

Finally, he is there.
Charlotte enters the apartment and hears Paula singing.
She crosses the living room quietly, so as not to disturb them.
But slowly enough to be seen.
The happiness of the moment makes her amnesic.
She forgets all about her disappointment in the café.
Nothing exists now but the ecstasy of seeing him again.
She goes to her room and sits on the bed, a docile little girl, and she hopes.

He opens the door of her room.
Without knocking, as always.
There is no border between them.
I wanted to apologize, he says right away.
For being so abrupt the other day.
She would like to tell him it doesn't matter, but she can't.

You must never expect anything from me.
Do you hear me?
Charlotte slowly nods.
If I'm rushed, I can't give anything.
I can't stand the idea of someone waiting for me.
Freedom is the survivors' slogan.
Alfred puts a hand on Charlotte's cheek.
And says: thank you.
Thank you for your drawings.
They are rough, naïve, unfinished.
But I love them for the power of their promise.

I love them because when I looked at them I could hear your voice.
I felt a kind of loss and uncertainty too.
Maybe even a hint of madness.
A gentle, docile madness, quiet and polite, but real.
Well, anyway.
That's what I wanted to tell you.
This could be the start of something beautiful between us.

Alfred shakes her hand and leaves.
He has understood that Charlotte gave herself completely to this.
For the first time, her drawings were dictated by necessity.
She didn't perform the work, she lived it.
This is a pivotal moment for her.
The man she loves put words to her frenzy.
She is intoxicated by what she has just experienced.
Now she knows where to go.
She knows where to hide, to shelter from the hatred.
Can she admit that she feels like an artist?
Artist.
She repeats this word.
Without really being able to define it.
Not that it matters.
Words do not always need a destination.
We can leave them behind us at the borders of feelings.
Running around headless in the vague zone.
And that is the privilege of artists: to live in confusion.

She paces her room.
Jumps on her bed, laughs like an idiot.
At this moment, her destiny seems fabulous to her.
Immoderation takes hold of her.

In the form of a fever.
A very real fever.
Charlotte is boiling hot.
That evening, her father is very worried.
He takes his daughter's temperature.
And notices the strange rhythm of her pulse.
He asks her numerous questions.
Did you go out half-dressed?
No.
Have you eaten anything unusual?
No.
Are you upset?
No.
Did someone insult you?
No, Father.

Charlotte reassures him, says she feels better.
It was just a momentary fit, everything's fine now.
Relieved, he hugs his daughter.
And realizes she is no longer hot.
What a strange phenomenon!
Once he is gone, she can't sleep.
Only she knows exactly what happened inside her body.

8

Charlotte wants to dazzle Alfred, that is certain.
But her hope is complex.
After feeling so strong, she falls back into doubt.
And spends her time putting herself down.

She cannot believe that he is really interested in her.
The man will inevitably realize how mediocre she is.
It goes without saying.
He will shine a light on her.
And burst out laughing as her con is exposed.

She wants to hide under the covers.
Suddenly, encouragement turns to fear.
She is terrified at the idea of seeing him again.
To see him is to risk disappointing him.
And he will abandon her: it is already written.
And that will be painful.
She is so afraid.
Is this how love feels?

The next time she sees Alfred, she is in a sullen mood.
Her body is home to an army of parentheses.
It's like there's a barrier around you, he says.
So he tries to make her laugh.
He tries absurdity, grotesquerie, outrageousness.
Charlotte gives a faint smile.
A breach in her tension.
No one ever tries to amuse her anymore.
For years, the atmosphere has been gloomy.
Every night, her father attempts to hide the humiliations of the day.
Paula pretends to think about her career.
About the day when she will be able to travel again.
Alfred is nothing like them.
He is a man out of nowhere.
You wouldn't even think he was living in 1938.

. . .

He arranges to meet her in a café again.
This is the second time they have broken the rules.
They are not allowed to be there, but they don't care.
It is an odd place.
Cats wander between tables.
And rub against customers' legs.
The atmosphere is like a waking dream.
With the dense smoke pouring from certain cigars.
I know all the cats here, says Alfred.
I've named them all after composers.
There's little Mahler, and over there is big fat Bach.
Look at Vivaldi purring.
And, of course, there's my favorite.
Beethoven.
You'll see, he's deaf as a post.
Call his name, ask him if he wants some milk: he won't turn round.
Charlotte, somewhat embarrassed, attempts to get the cat's attention.
It's no use: Beethoven ignores her.
He blinks, sleepily.

Alfred continues to humanize the cats.
This gives him the chance to mention Schubert again.
The two of them return to the subject of *Death and the Maiden*.
The piece obsesses them both in a similar way.
Alfred launches into a monologue on the life of a musician.
Schubert wasn't exactly a ladies' man, you know.
He was small and he considered himself deformed.
Despite all his compositions, he knew very little about sex.
He was practically a virgin when he died.
You can tell, sometimes, when you listen to him.
His Hungarian melodies are a virgin's music.

There's no flesh in Schubert.
And then he slept with a prostitute.
Who gave him a fatal disease.
His death throes lasted for years.
Poor Schubert, eh?
Still, at least there's a cat named after him now.
That's a form of posterity.

Charlotte is dazed.
She is thinking about Schubert, of course.
But what burns in her mind is a more personal question.
What about you?
What about me?
Have you been with many women, Alfred?
Oh, women . . .
Yes, I've known some.
That is how he answers her.
Evasively.
And then, suddenly, he becomes more explicit.
Yes, I've been with women.
I can't tell you how many.
But all of them were important.
It can never be insignificant.
A woman naked in front of me.
A woman opening her mouth.
I respected every one of them.
Even the most fleeting.

9

Charlotte forgets the rest of the world.
Her family's anxieties.

When she gets home, her father is waiting for her in the living room.
Is he relieved or furious?
Probably some combination of the two.
After a while, Albert starts yelling.
Where were you?!
Don't you ever think about us?
Didn't it occur to you that we'd be worried, desperate?
Charlotte lowers her head.
She knows that anything can happen at night.
If she'd been stopped, they might have deported her.
They might have beaten her, tortured her, raped her, killed her.
She apologizes, but she cannot manage to cry.
She merely stammers that she was daydreaming.
This is the first excuse that comes to mind.
Paula walks over to calm down the situation.
Never do that to us again, she says.
If you must daydream, come home to do it.

Charlotte promises to be careful.
But that is no kind of life for a young woman.
She is twenty-one years old and she wants to be free.
She can't even breathe without planning it in advance.
All spontaneity is forbidden.
But ultimately, nothing else matters tonight.

She is happy.
She could live in prison, as long as he was there with her.
As she kisses her father, a smile appears.
Charlotte's face lights up.
She tries to stop herself giggling.

Paula notices this, without understanding.
It is the first time she has seen Charlotte like this.
Usually, she is so enclosed.
Two minutes ago, she was on the verge of tears.
She apologized sincerely.
And now she can't stop smiling.

Sorry.
Sorry, Charlotte repeats, as she runs to her room.
Paula and Albert stare at her, warily.
Disturbed, even.
After all, insanity runs in the family.

10

A few days later, they meet again in Wannsee.
A magical part of Berlin, with three lakes.
The gray sky has kept the crowds away.
At this moment, they are alone.
And Charlotte is free.
This time, she has warned her parents: I'll be at Barbara's house.

They sit on a bench where they are not allowed to sit.
Their bodies hide the sign.

NUR FÜR ARIER: only for Aryans.
With Alfred, Charlotte feels capable of daring.
I can't stand our era anymore, she says.
This era that seems to go on forever.

A few yards from their bench is the Villa Marlier.
They admire the beauty and elegance of that building.
On January 20, 1942, high-ranking Nazis will meet here.
For a little work meeting organized by Reinhard Heydrich.
History knows it as *the Wannsee Conference*.
In two hours, they will put the finishing touches to the machinery of the Final Solution.
The methods of liquidation defined.
Good, it's all sorted.
Excellent work, gentlemen.
Now let us relax in the lounge.
A very fine Cognac is served.
They sip it with the satisfaction of a duty accomplished.

Today, the men from that meeting are frozen in photographs.
They are immortal, or rather: they must never be forgotten.
The villa has become a place of memorial.
I visited it one gloriously sunny day in July 2004.
You can walk through the horror.
The long table used for the meeting is frightening.
As if the objects had taken part in the crime.
The place will forever be charged with terror.
So this is what it means, when *a chill runs down your spine*.
I had never understood that expression before.
The physical manifestation of an invisible icy finger.
Tracing the vertebrae in your back.

11

Alfred takes Charlotte's hand.
Let's go for a boat ride.
But it looks like it's going to rain, she replies.
So?
Is rain really a danger in Germany?
They climb into the small boat.
And let it drift across the wide lake.
The sky darkens, like a room after sunset.
Charlotte lies down.
That way, she can take more pleasure in the movements of the water.
She could drift on like this forever.
Her position reminds Alfred of a work by Michelangelo.
A sculpture entitled *Night*.
There he sits, facing the ideal.
The storm begins to rumble.
The world is cleansed by thunder, he says.
He moves closer, to kiss her.

Lost in their kiss, they do not hear.
A man yelling at them to return.
They are crazy to stay out in the deluge.
Finally, they come back to reality.
The boat is full of water.
They must quickly row back to the shore.
With her hands, Charlotte tries to shovel the water from the boat.
While Alfred works the oars.
Thankfully, they make it to the banks of the lake.

And climb out, laughing.
The boat owner staring at them aghast.
Then they run through the park to the exit.
The rain turning them into fugitives.

12

She agrees to go to his place.
Soaked to the bone, they enter the hovel.
The décor doesn't matter.
There are piles of books on the floor.
He tells her to get undressed so she doesn't catch cold.
She obeys without even thinking.

She thought she would be afraid, but the opposite is true.
As her desire grows, so does her boldness.
He pronounces her name: Charlotte.
Several times.
She likes her name in his mouth.
Charlotte again.

She stands naked.
He kisses her all over her body.
A promenade lost between sweetness and torture.
And yet his crazy wanderings are so precise.
Already they are touching the sensual consecration.
Charlotte breathes yes yes yes and arches her back.
Alfred, my love.

It is his turn to strip.
And they move toward the bed.

They have passed from one world to another.
Without the slightest transition.
Some uncertainties end as inevitabilities.
They embrace and it burns.
Desire almost biting.
He observes the young woman, naked and open.
A proof of life, a hard slap in the face.
He can speak, dream, sing, write, create, die.
But this is the only instant that is worth all the suffering.
Vice in the guise of innocence.
Nothing else matters.
Alfred is doubly aware of this.
He is an artist, and he is a man.

Just as she was feeling strong, it is devastation.
Charlotte's body starts to tremble.
There are shadows on her face.
It's the past, fleeing.
Frightened away by the total hegemony of now.
She abandons herself, with even greater strength.
So speaks her happiness.

Part Five

1

Nineteen thirty-eight is the year of the disintegration.
Charlotte's final hopes will be smashed to pieces.
A terrible humiliation awaits her.

Every spring, there is a contest at the Academy.
The students each produce one work, based on a specified subject.
It is the highlight of the year.
The moment when the prizes and honors are distributed.
Ludwig Bartning's admiration of Charlotte is increasing.
He is glad that he fought for her acceptance.
During the past few months, her progress has been meteoric.
It is not a question of technique.
Though of course her drawing is becoming more refined, more precise.
What strikes him is the assuredness of his protégée.
She uses every exercise to develop her voice.
Singular, strange, poetic, feverish.
Her drawing expresses who she is.
Her strength is not obvious at first glance.
Her distinctiveness is hidden somewhere, beneath an array of colors.
Ludwig sees it, though.
Something he hasn't seen in years.
Nobody knows, except him.
There is a genius in their midst.

The contest is always anonymous.
Only once the prizes have been assigned are their authors revealed.

The professors sit around a table.
Unanimously, they choose one picture.
For once, the decision is made quickly.
This is always an exciting moment.
Each teacher hazards a guess.
A few names are uttered.
But deep down, nobody really knows.
The victor has covered their tracks.
No one recognizes it as the work of any student.
Now the time has come to discover the artist's identity.
Next to the drawing is an envelope.
The professor who opens it says nothing.
The others lean toward him: so?
He looks at his colleagues, as if timing a dramatic pause.
Before making the announcement in a hollow voice.
The first prize is awarded to Charlotte Salomon.

Instantly the room becomes tense.
It is impossible that she should receive this prize.
The ceremony attracts too much attention.
People would talk about the Jewification of the art school.
The prizewinner herself would be too exposed.
She would immediately become a target.
She might be imprisoned.
Ludwig Bartning understands the gravity of the situation.
Someone suggests: why don't we vote again?
No, that would be too unfair.
We can deprive her of her prize, but not of her victory.
So says her ardent defender.
He fights for her, as best he can.
His support for Charlotte could prove fatal for him.

Everything comes out in the end; nothing remains secret.
But his courage is rewarded.
Because he succeeds in getting the prize validated.

One hour later, he waits for Charlotte in the lobby.
He signals to her with his hand.
She approaches, shy as always.
He doesn't know how to begin.
This should be a joyous moment.
And yet he looks distraught.
Finally, he tells her that she won the contest.
But doesn't give her time to express her happiness.
He undercuts the news with the professors' decision.
She will not be allowed to receive her trophy.
Charlotte is shaken by two contradictory emotions.
Joy and pain.
She accepts that she cannot show herself.
For two years now, she has been a shadow.
But today, it is so unjust.

He explains that her work will be rewarded.
But someone else must receive the prize.
Who? asks Charlotte.
I don't know, Ludwig replies.
Barbara.
That is who Charlotte proposes.
Barbara.
Barbara, are you sure? he asks.
I'm certain.
Why her?
She already has everything, says Charlotte, so she must be given even more.

• • •

Three days later, Barbara is on the stage.
Three days of tears for Charlotte.
The blonde prizewinner is all smiles.
She accepts this prize, which is not hers.
Without any apparent embarrassment.
She looks as if she really believes she is the winner.
She thanks her parents and her friends.
She should also thank her country, thinks Charlotte.
Humiliated, watching this charade.

In the middle of the ceremony, she runs off.
Ludwig watches her leave.
He wants to catch her, give her more support.
But she is gone so fast.
She barely hears the applause ring out.
As she is leaving the Academy.

She runs all the way to her apartment.
In her room, she lies motionless on the bed.
Then gets to her feet and crumples up her drawings.
Some of them she rips to shreds.
Drawn by the noise, Paula enters the room.
But what are you doing?
What's going on?
I am never going back to the Academy, she says coldly.

2

Charlotte spends whole days sitting on her bed.
Alfred is at the center of her thoughts.
It is becoming an obsession.
Later, she will draw his face over and over again.
Hundreds of sketches of her love.
She will also remember all his words.
The present begins to take the form of always.

After their first night, he disappeared again.
No news at all.
And he is no longer giving lessons to her stepmother.
Charlotte must accept his silence.
You must never expect anything from me, he said.
But it's so hard.
It's beyond her endurance.
She dresses to go out.
And tells her stepmother that she's leaving to see a friend.

It is always dangerous to go out late at night.
She could have her papers checked, of course.
But the risk is not so great.
Sometimes a smile will do instead of papers.
Particularly when you look like an Aryan.
Which is true for Charlotte.
Her chestnut hair is pale, and so are her eyes.
Without this bad blood, she would be free to live.
She walks through the black night.

Until she finds herself outside his apartment.
She hides in the darkness, heart pounding feverishly.
She doesn't want to go up, just to see him.
Anyway, she knows he wouldn't forgive her for forcing herself on him.
She has promised never to do that.
To respect his freedom completely.
But why does she never hear from him?
Maybe he lied about his feelings?
The night with her was awful and disappointing.
And he doesn't dare tell her so.
That must be it.
Has to be.
Maybe he's even forgotten her name.
Though he loved saying it so much: Charlotte.

At that moment, she sees him through the window.
The mere sight of his shadow overwhelms her.
The room is lit by a candle.
Alfred appears and disappears in time with its flickerings.
This makes reality seem as improbable as a dream.
And then a figure interrupts the scene.
A woman seems to wander into the living room.
She is doggedly searching for something.
Then, suddenly, she rushes toward Alfred.
Charlotte has stopped breathing.
And yet she knows that Alfred is free.
He never promised to belong to her.
They are not a couple.
These are moments outside everyday life.

It starts to rain again.
It's always like this: whenever they come close, it rains.

The sky clouds over for their meetings.
Charlotte cannot move, to protect herself from the rain.
Alfred looks extremely annoyed.
He grabs the woman firmly by her arms.
And ushers her to the front door.

They are outside now, a few yards from Charlotte.
The girl is begging him, but for what?
Probably she is saying that it's impossible to leave in such rain.
Alfred insists, pushing her away angrily.
She gives up, head lowered.
He stays there unmoving, probably relieved.
After a while, Alfred turns.
And sees Charlotte.

He signals her over.
She walks slowly across the empty street.
What are you doing there? he asks coldly.
He knows the answer.
I wanted to see you, I hadn't heard anything.
I was going to write, you shouldn't rush me.
He hesitates for an instant before asking her up.
Charlotte's heart races.
She is about to re-enter her kingdom.
The floor of this seedy room.
Where he will perhaps make love to her again.

For the moment, she sits on the edge of a chair.
Frozen with embarrassment.
She apologizes for having broken their rule.
She can tell he is very annoyed.

She should never have come.
It's all over, and it's her fault.
Any time she's happy, she has to ruin it all.
So why does she keep digging by asking:
Who was that woman?
Don't ask me questions, Charlotte.
Never, do you hear me?
Never.
But, just this once, I will answer you.
That woman is my fiancée.
She was picking up her things, that's all.
She looked upset, says Charlotte.
So?
Must I be responsible for the sufferings of others?
After a pause, he adds: never do that again.
What?
Coming here, like that.
If you oppress me, you will lose me.
I'm sorry, I'm sorry, she repeats.
Before daring to add: but, do you love her?
Who?
Well, that woman . . .
Don't ask me anything.
Life is too short for nonsense like that.
If you must know, we are separated.
She came to fetch a book she'd forgotten.
But if I had been with her, that wouldn't have changed anything.

Charlotte is no longer sure she understands what he's saying.
Not that it matters.
All she knows is: she feels good here, with him.

How many times do people feel like that?
Once, twice, never.
She shivers with cold.
Her teeth chatter.
Finally, he moves toward her to warm her up.

3

Where was the logic in his silence?
When he seems so thrilled to see her again.
He spends a long time contemplating her.
As if he is responsible for this moment.
As if he did everything he could to find her again.
It's incomprehensible.
Charlotte becomes lost in a labyrinth of futile thoughts.
But it makes no difference.
She wants to give herself to him, and that's all.
He is more brutal than last time.
He pulls her hair with a lover's strength.
Charlotte's mouth opens.
And travels down her beloved's torso.
He is touched by the energy she puts into giving him pleasure.
She can't get enough of it now.
It is hope that crosses her throat.
She seems to understand so perfectly what he likes.

Charlotte falls asleep, happy.
He looks at her again, a savage child calmed.
So he had to survive for this moment.
Alfred plunges his face into Charlotte's hair.

An image comes to his mind.
A painting by Munch:
Man's Head in Woman's Hair.

He stays like that for a moment, before getting up.
He walks over to his desk and starts to write.
Poems, or simply isolated sentences.
A few pages inspired by beauty.
Charlotte awakes.
Did she hear the din of her lover's thoughts?
She moves toward the written words.
Alfred says: it's for you.
You have to read it while imagining a piece by Schubert.
Yes, yes, yes, she says, thinking about the *Impromptus.*
She starts to read, and the words come to her.
It is not always the reader who has to go toward the sentences.
Especially not with Alfred's, so powerful and indomitable.
Charlotte mentally underlines each one.
He writes about her and him, and it's the history of a world.
It's Schubert's impromptu in G-flat major.
They are the minor of hideaways and the major of true lovers.

She tries to pick up a page, but Alfred stops her.
He grabs the whole sheaf.
And throws them on the fire.
Charlotte screams.
Why?!
Suddenly.
In a second.
When it must have taken him hours to write.
She cries.

She is in despair.
No one had ever written such words for her before.
And now they are all gone.
He takes her in his arms.
He says they exist, and will always exist.
Not in a material form.
But in memory.
They will exist with the music of Schubert.
The music we do not hear, but which is there.
He goes on, explaining the beauty of the gesture to her.
The essential thing is that those words were written.
The rest doesn't matter.
We must not leave evidence for the dogs anymore.
We must put away our books and our memories inside us.

4

In France, at that very moment, a man gets up.
He looks at the reflection in his bedroom mirror.
For a long time now, he hasn't been able to recognize himself.
He can barely even say his own name: Herschel Grynszpan.

A seventeen-year-old Polish Jew, he lives in forced exile in Paris.
He has just received a despairing letter from his sister.
His entire family has been expelled.
Without warning, they must leave their country.
Now they are in a refugee camp.
For too long, Grynszpan's life has been nothing but humiliation.
His existence is like a rat's, he thinks.

So, on that morning of November 7, 1938, he writes:
I must protest, so that the whole world hears my protest.

Armed with a pistol, he enters the German embassy.
Claiming he has an important document, he finds himself in a diplomat's
   office.
Later, it will be said that this was a settling of personal scores.
A private, sexual affair with an unhappy ending.
Does it really matter?
In this moment, all that counts is the hatred.
The third secretary, Ernst Vom Rath, is pale.
There can be no doubting the young man's determination.
And yet, the would-be killer is trembling.
His palms are clammy.
The scene seems to go on forever.
But it doesn't.
He pulls the trigger now.
He shoots the German at point-blank range.
Several shots, one after another.
The diplomat's head smashes into the desk.
Cracking his skull.
Blood pours onto the floorboards.
A red pool forms around the assassin.
Officers burst in.
The killer does not try to get away.

The news soon reaches Berlin.
The Fuhrer flies into a rage.
Vengeance must be immediate.
How dare he?

Quick, crush this vermin.
And then, no.
Not him.
All of them.
It's a race that's to blame.
Spreading.
Vom Rath was killed by all the Jews.
Pleasure mingles with rage.
The pleasure of reprisals.

5

The Salomon family is eating lunch in silence.
There's a knock at the door.
Charlotte looks at her father.
Every sound is a menace.
It cannot be otherwise.
They all remain seated around the table.
Without moving, immobilized by fear.
More knocking.
Harder, more determined.
They must do something.
If they don't, the door will be smashed down.
Finally, Albert gets to his feet.
Two men in dark suits stand outside.
Albert Salomon?
Yes.
Please follow us.
Where are we going?
Don't ask questions.

Can I take a few things?
There's no point, just hurry up.

Paula tries to intervene.
Albert signals her to keep quiet.
Better to avoid a scene.
They'll fire at the least sign of resistance.
They only want him, so at least that's something.
Probably for an interrogation.
It won't last long.
They'll realize that he's a war hero.
He gave his blood for Germany.

Albert puts on his coat and his hat.
And turns around to kiss his wife and daughter goodbye.
Hurry up!
His kisses are fleeting, stolen.
He leaves the apartment, without looking back.
Charlotte and Paula hug each other tight.
They don't know why he was taken.
They don't know where he's going.
They don't know how long it will be.
They don't know anything.
Kafka wrote about this in *The Trial*.
The hero, Joseph K., is arrested without reason.
Just like Albert, he prefers not to resist.
*The only judicious attitude consists in accommodating oneself to the
    way things are.*
So that's it.
It's "the way things are."
There is nothing to be done against the way things are.

But how far does that way go?
The process seems irreversible.
Everything has already been written in the novel.
Josef K. will be killed like a dog.
As if *the shame must outlive him*.

6

Without any explanation, Albert is thrown into Sachsenhausen.
A concentration camp to the north of Berlin.
He is penned up in a cramped room with other men.
Albert recognizes some of them.
They exchange a few words to reassure each other.
In their heads, they play out pitiful scenes of optimism.
But none of them really believes it anymore.
It's gone much too far now.
They've been left here to die, nothing to eat or drink.
Why does no one come to see them?
How can they be treated like this by their compatriots?
After several hours, some officers turn up.
They open the door of the shack.
A few protests are raised.
The rebels are immediately seized.
They are led to another part of the camp.
They will not be seen again.

The officers explain to the prisoners that they are going to be
    interrogated.
They must form a line.
Standing in the cold, they wait for hours.

Some are too old or too sick to hold out.

Those who collapse are transported somewhere else.

They will not be seen again either.

The Nazis are not yet executing people in broad daylight.

The weak and the defiant are shot in the backyard.

Albert positions himself in the middle of the line of dignified men.

Yes, they are dignified.

The determination not to offer up their pain, on top of everything else,
   is palpable.

It is the only thing you can keep.

When you have nothing left.

The desire to stand up straight.

His turn comes.

He finds himself facing a young man who could be his son.

You're a doctor, he snorts.

Yes.

No surprise there, that's a real Jew's job.

Well, you're not going to twiddle your thumbs here, you lazy bastard!

How can anyone call Albert lazy?

He has worked all his life like a man possessed.

Striving to make medical breakthroughs.

If this shit-for-brains soldier doesn't die of an ulcer, it will be thanks to him.

Albert lowers his eyes: it is too much to bear.

Look at me! shouts the young Nazi.

Look at me when I'm talking to you, vermin!

Albert lifts his head, like a puppet.

Takes the sheet of paper that is handed to him.

And reads on it the number of his dormitory, and his serial number.

He no longer has the right to a name.

. . .

The first days are torture.
Albert is not used to physical work.
He is out on his feet, but he knows he must keep going.
If he falls, he risks leaving.
Leaving for that place from where no one ever comes back.
Exhaustion wipes out his ability to think.
In certain moments, he doesn't know anything at all anymore.
He doesn't know where he is, who he is.
As when you wake from a nightmare.
And it takes you several seconds to return to reality.
Albert stays in this zone for hours on end.
His consciousness wandering.

As for Charlotte and Paula, they are exhausted by lucidity.
The lack of news eats away at them.
Like hundreds of other women, they stand outside police stations.
In front of the building, there is a huge crowd of female protesters.
Where are our husbands?
Where are our fathers?
They beg for information.
For some proof that they're alive.
Charlotte manages to enter one of the offices.
She is carrying a warm blanket.
I would like to deliver this to my father, she pleads.
The officers force themselves not to laugh.
What's his name? a Nazi finally asks.
Albert Salomon.
All right, you can go now, we'll take care of it.
But I would like to take it to him myself, please.
That's impossible.

No visits are allowed for the moment.

Charlotte knows she must not insist.

If she wants the blanket to reach her father, she must keep quiet.

She leaves in silence.

A few seconds after this, the officers burst out laughing.

Ah, that's so sweet!

Does the little Jewish girl want to take care of her daddy-waddy?

Ah . . . Oh . . . Ah . . . they snigger.

As they wipe their muddy boots on the blanket.

7

Weeks pass.

The most terrible rumors circulate about the fate of the men.

Hundreds have died, it is said.

Paula and Charlotte still haven't heard anything.

Is Albert even alive?

The opera singer does everything she can to liberate her husband.

She still has a few admirers among the Nazi hierarchy.

They will see what they can do to help her.

It's complicated: no one is being released.

Please, please, I beg you.

She implores them constantly.

Alfred is there, during the unbearable days of waiting.

He distracts them as best he can.

Whenever Paula looks away, he embraces Charlotte.

But he too is taut with anxiety.

The arrests have been aimed at the elite, above all.

Intellectuals, artists, professors, doctors.

Soon, they will attack those who have nothing.
And he will be first in line.

Everyone is trying to flee.
But where?
How?
The borders are closed.
Only Charlotte is able to leave.
If you are under twenty-two, it's possible.
You do not need a passport to leave the country.
She still has a few months.
Her grandparents have heard about the latest incidents.
In their letters, they beg Charlotte to join them.
It's a paradise here, in the South of France.
She can't stay in Germany any longer.
It's becoming too much of a risk.
Paula shares this opinion.
But Charlotte can't leave like that.
Without seeing her father again.
Although, truth be told, this is an excuse.
She has already made her decision.
She will never leave Germany.
For the simple reason that she will never leave Alfred.

Paula's efforts are finally rewarded.
After four months, Albert is released from the camp.
He goes home, but he is not the same man.
Horribly thin, wild-eyed, he lies on the bed.
Paula draws the curtains, and lets him sleep.
Charlotte is in shock.
She stays close to him for several hours.
Fighting against the despair that threatens to overwhelm her.

. . .

She is worried by her father's labored breathing.

Watching over him, she feels a strange emotion.

Of being able to protect him from death.

Slowly, he regains his strength.

But hardly speaks at all.

Sometimes he sleeps all day.

This man who used to stay up working all night.

One morning, when he opens his eyes, he calls for his wife.

Paula comes right away.

What is it, my love?

He opens his mouth, but no sound emerges.

He can't say what he wants to say.

At last, he emits a sound that is a name: Charlotte . . .

What about Charlotte?

Charlotte . . . she must . . . leave.

Paula knows how much those words hurt him.

More than ever, he needs his daughter close to him.

But he knows now that there is no hope.

He was on the front line of the horror.

She must flee, quickly.

While it is still possible.

8

Charlotte refuses, of course.

She doesn't want to leave, she can't leave.

The others insist: there's no time to lose.

No, I don't want to leave you, she repeats.

As soon as we've gotten our fake papers, we'll join you, they assure her.

No, I don't want to, no, I don't want to.
Paula and Albert don't understand.
Only Alfred knows the truth.
He finds her attitude absurd, excessive.
No love is worth risking death for, he thinks.
And it is death that awaits them here.

Charlotte doesn't listen.
She listens only to herself; to her heart, in other words.
She repeats over and over: I can't leave you.
The pain would be unbearable. Don't you understand how much I love you?
He takes her hands.
Of course he understands.
He loves her feverish, fanatical temperament.
The beauty of a love stronger than fear.
But that is no longer the point.
He has no other choice but to threaten her.
If you don't leave, I will never see you again.

She knows Alfred so well.
These are not empty words.
If she doesn't leave Germany, he will vanish from her life.
It is the only blackmail she can understand.
He, too, promises to meet her in the South of France.
But how will you manage it?
I have contacts, he tells her.
How to believe him?
She can't anymore.
She doesn't want to leave her life behind.
She was born here.
Why must she face up to yet more suffering?

She would rather die than leave.
She seriously considers it.

Her father asks to see her.
He takes her hand, feebly.
And repeats: please, you must leave.
A tear escapes his eye.
This is the first time she has seen her father weep.
The world wavers on his face.
Charlotte takes out her handkerchief to dry the tear.
Albert suddenly thinks of Franziska.
This scene reminds him of their first meeting.
When she took his handkerchief to blow his nose.
While he was in the middle of an operation, close to the battlefield.
The two scenes resonate within him.
Mother and daughter reunited by a single gesture.
And he realizes that it is the end of the movement.
With this gesture, Charlotte is agreeing to leave.

9

There are ways and means of leaving the country.
Paula asks the grandparents to write fake letters.
Saying that the grandmother is about to die.
She is very sick, and wants to see her granddaughter again.
Armed with this proof, Charlotte goes to the French Consulate.
And obtains a short-stay visa.
So her papers are now in order.
She moves through her final hours like an automaton.
She stands motionless facing her suitcase.

A very small suitcase, because this is supposed to be a short trip.
She can take so little with her.
She is forced to choose between her memories.
Which books should she take?
Which drawing?
Finally she decides to take one of Paula's records.
A version of *Carmen* that she loves so much.
A reminder of happier days.

Alone, she goes to the cemetery to say goodbye to her mother.
For months, she believed that she had become an angel.
She imagined her in the sky above Berlin.
Flying on wings of desire.
It's all over now.
Charlotte is facing reality.
The sky is empty.
And her mother's body is decomposing here.
Her bones locked away in this tomb.

Does she remember the warmth, at least?
When her mother used to take her in her arms.
And sing to her.
No, nothing now seems ever to have existed.
Except her first memories, in this very place.
When she read her name on her aunt's grave.
Charlotte, the first Charlotte.
And now the two sisters are forever reunited.
She puts a white rose on each headstone.
And leaves.

. . .

Standing in front of her father, she weeps.
He is too weak to accompany her to the station.
They comfort each other with the word *soon*.
Soon, they will see each other again.
Soon, everything will be all right.
Her father is so reserved.
Tenderness makes him uneasy.
But today, he keeps breathing in his daughter.
As if he wanted to hold on to a treasure.
And hide it for as long as possible inside him.
Charlotte kisses her father for a long time.
And leaves her mark on him.
Not lipstick.
Just the imprint of her lips, pressed so hard against him.

10

Policemen patrol the station platform.
Charlotte, standing with Paula and Alfred, must hide her feelings.
An outpouring of emotion would attract attention.
The three of them would be interrogated.
Why is this girl crying so much?
She's only leaving for a week, isn't she?
So no, she must not endanger their plan.
She must remain dignified and calm.
As she casually tears out her own heart.
Charlotte wants to scream with pain.
But it's impossible.
She is leaving everything behind.
Her father, Paula, her mother's tomb.

She is leaving her memories, her life, her childhood.
But most of all, she is leaving him.
Her great, her only love.
This man who is everything to her.
Her lover and her soul.

Alfred has trouble concealing his emotion.
Usually so chatty, he is silent today.
What he feels is too new to be defined.
The smoke from the train envelops the scene in mist.
More than ever, the platform resembles a shore.
The perfect backdrop for the final moment.
Alfred puts his mouth close to Charlotte's ear.
She thinks he's going to say: I love you.
But no.
He whispers something more important.
A phrase she will think about constantly.
Which will become the essence of her obsession.

May you never forget that I believe in you.

Part Six

1

Charlotte watches the platform shrink to nothing.
Head poking through the window, face whipped by the wind.
Inside the carriage, a cold voice speaks.
Please close the window, miss.
Charlotte obeys and sits in her seat.
She holds back the tears as the landscape speeds past.
Some of the passengers speak to her, and she answers briefly.
Does all she can to drive the conversation toward a dead end.
They must think her impolite, even arrogant.
But who cares what they think.
It doesn't matter anymore.

At the French border, her papers are checked.
She is interrogated about the reasons for her trip.
I'm going to visit my sick grandma.
The customs officer smiles at her.
It's not difficult to play the nice Aryan girl.
Inside the skin of that character, everything is wonderful.
She lives in a world where no one ever spits on her.
Barbara's world.
A world where people love you, favor you, honor you.
They even wish her good luck.

The train arrives in Paris.
For a few seconds, she basks in the wonder.

The wonder of that name: Paris.
The promise of France.
But she has to run so she won't miss her connection.
She jumps aboard the train just in time.
Again, people try to talk to her.
But she signals to them that she doesn't understand.
That is the advantage of being in a foreign country.
As soon as people know you don't speak the language.
They give up trying to speak to you.

She is fascinated by the beauty of the fields the train passes.
There are more colors in this country, she thinks.
She knows many painters have followed this path.
To find the light in the South of France.
That spellbinding yellow light.
Will she feel the same sensation?
With a black veil hanging constantly before her eyes.
Her stomach is starting to ache.
She is surprised by her body's awakening.
If she is hungry, that means everything she's experiencing is real.
The woman next to her gives her an apple.
Starving, she devours it.
She even eats the core.
The woman is surprised.
She was not expecting such an appetite.
She is almost scared of Charlotte now.
Just because she ate an apple too fast.

On arriving in Nice, Charlotte inquires at the counter.
She shows her sheet of paper: Villefranche-sur-Mer.
They point to a bus, and she sits down near the front.

She is afraid of getting lost, of getting off at the wrong stop.
She shows her sheet of paper to the bus driver.
Thirty minutes later, he signals to her that she has arrived.
She climbs off the bus, saying a word in French: *merci*.
Once she is alone, she repeats it to herself: *merci*.
She likes the feeling of speaking another language.
Especially as her own language is ruined.
Exile is not only a question of place.
That *merci* is a form of shelter.

Once again, she asks a woman for directions.
This one knows all about Ottilie Moore's house.
Like everyone around here, presumably.
The rich American lady is famous in this region.
She provides a home for many orphans.
She gives them dance and circus classes.
All Charlotte has to do is take this winding road.
She can't miss the house.

It's hot, and the path is steep.
This is the final stage of a very long journey.
Soon, she will kiss her grandparents.
She wasn't able to tell them what day she was arriving.
They will be surprised by her appearance.
She hasn't seen them in so long.
Have they changed much?
But, above all, it is they who will not recognize her.
When they left, she was a teenager, and now she's a young woman.
Despite her sorrow, she is intensely excited.

.   .   .

Finally she arrives at the Ermitage.
It is a magnificent abode, perched on a hill.
With a garden that looks like paradise.
Behind the foliage, she sees children running.
She hears their laughter too.
Charlotte is not yet capable of ringing the bell at the gate.
It is a new life that awaits her here.
All she need do is walk a few yards.
And she will find herself in the unknown.

Something holds her back.
It is a force behind her.
She almost has the impression that her name is being called.
The force turns her around.
And she discovers the majestic sparkle of the Mediterranean.
Charlotte has never seen anything so beautiful in her life.

2

A few minutes later, she is in the garden.
Surrounded by children celebrating her arrival.
Ottilie Moore asks them to calm down.
They must let Charlotte rest: she is exhausted.
Vittoria Bravi, the cook, makes some lemonade.
In the middle of all this warmth, the grandparents stand immobile.
The grandmother has tears in her eyes.
Charlotte feels as if she's been sucked into the whirlwind that encircles her.
She is not used to answering so many questions.
Did she have a good trip?
How does she feel?

How are her parents?
How is Germany?
She stammers that she doesn't know.
She has barely spoken a word in the last two days.
And besides, she is so lacking in confidence.
Being watched like this makes her very anxious.
And there is something else that bothers her.
She feels guilty that she is there.

Ottilie senses this unease.
Come, Charlotte, I'll show you to your room.
They leave the garden, watched by surprised faces.
She's still as melancholy as ever, the grandfather concludes.
Before adding: just like her mother.
The grandmother glares at him.
She does not want to hear those words.
She does not want to grasp their implication.
And yet, he is right.
She was struck by it too.
Charlotte's resemblance to Franziska is incredible.
In the features of her face, of course, but also in her attitude.
They share the same sadness.
What should be a source of joy no longer is.
In fact, it's the beginning of fear.

3

Charlotte sleeps for a long time.
And wakes up in the middle of the night.
Barefoot, she walks through the garden on that first night.

Wearing a white nightgown, with a sensation of freedom.
The sky is pale blue, almost yellowish, with stars.
She touches the trunks of trees, inhales the scents of flowers.
Then she lies down in the grass.
In the immensity of the sky, she sees Alfred's face.
With clouds in his mouth.
And she lets herself be overwhelmed by desire.

Days pass, and Charlotte still doesn't talk much.
The others find her very reserved.
The children nickname her: the silent one.
They would like to play with her.
For now, she only agrees to draw them.
Ottilie thinks she has an exceptional talent.
She even says: we have a genius in the house.

The American lady is constantly encouraging her to paint.
She will buy her drawings, to help her make a living from her work.
She will make arrangements to find paper for her, in spite of the war.
This woman's generosity seems limitless.
In the photographs of her that remain, she is always smiling.
And there is a hint of extravagance in her expression.

They remember her, in Villefranche-sur-Mer.
In 1968, her incredible home was demolished.
To make way for one of those so-called prestige apartment buildings.
The garden was partly replaced by a swimming pool.
Only the two tall pine trees survived.
With the swing between them.
Around the apartment building now, there is a high wall.
To prevent intruders entering.

Intruders and French writers fascinated by Charlotte Salomon.
How to get in?
It's impossible.
This place, once so welcoming, is now inaccessible.

A man, seeing me standing there idiotically, offers to help me.
We speak a bit, and I ask him his name.
It is Michel Veziano.
He seems unsurprised when I explain to him the aim of my research.
He tells me a European came here on the same quest.
Yes, that is the word he uses: European.
Three or four years ago, roughly.
So I am not the only one in search of Charlotte.
We form a small and scattered sect.
Exhausted disciples saved by Michel.
I am not sure if this is reassuring or unbearable.
What was the other man's name?
Michel does not remember.
Did he really exist?
I would like to know everyone who loves Charlotte.

At this point in my reflections, the security gate opens.
A woman in a car comes out.
I quickly leave Michel to go see her.
Hello madame, I'm a writer . . .
She knows who Ottilie Moore was, because she has lived here since 1968.
As I am about to start asking her questions, she becomes angry.
No, you can't stay here!
And anyway, the security guard won't let you in!
Go away, you have no business here!
She is a sour, frightened, stupid old woman.

I speak to her softly.
I would just like to walk in the garden for five minutes.
I show her a book with old photographs in it.
She refuses to look at it.
Go away, go away, or I'll call the security guard!
I don't understand.
Why is she so hostile?

I decide to give up.
It's not all that important.
Nothing remains of the past here, after all.
Thanks to this woman, though, I was able to taste a little bit of 1943.
What a strange coincidence.
Because it is here that hatred will soon strike at Charlotte.

4

Charlotte spends hours hoping that Alfred will turn up.
She is forever imagining her beloved's arrival.
Like a god appearing out of the blue.
But he doesn't come.
To bring him to life, she reconstructs their conversations.
Word for word: she has forgotten nothing.
Her precision is the heart's memory.
Who can know Charlotte's despair?
She is a young woman alone with her demon.
Sometimes she smiles at people, so they will leave her in peace.
Ottilie Moore worries especially about the grandmother.
She was so happy before.
Often laughing, curious about everything.

She asks Charlotte to cheer her up.
It's like asking the grayness to light up the blackness.
Grandmother and granddaughter understand each other.
Their hearts beat in the same way.
As if they'd been wrapped up in cloth.
Struggling, muffled, making no noise inside the body.
Guiltily, the way survivors do everything.

They walk by the sea.
The sound of the waves allows them not to speak.
Better to stay silent, anyway.
The news is getting ever more tragic.
Germany has just invaded Poland.
France and England have declared war.
The grandmother sits on a bench.
She is finding it hard to breathe.
For years, she has fought to stay alive.
Since the deaths of her daughters, every day is a battle.
But it has become pointless.
The war will destroy everything.

They call Dr Moridis.
An eminent local figure.
Feted for his charisma, his humanism.
He charges the rich more, and the poor less.
It's said that he's looked after some passing celebrities.
Errol Flynn, Martine Carol, even Edith Piaf.
He cared for Ottilie after her car accident.
That was in the early 1930s.
Since then, they have grown very close.
So the American lady turns to him.
Would he try to save Charlotte's grandmother?

. . .

And so the doctor comes to the Ermitage.
Charlotte greets him and leads him to the old lady's bedside.
What is his first impression, when he meets her?
Impossible to know.
All the same, I will try to seize that moment.
It seems so crucial to me.
The entrance of Dr. Moridis in the story.
This man will prove very important for Charlotte.
I try to see him in the garden.
In the photographs that his daughter showed me, he looks huge.
I imagine the children lifting their heads to stare up at him.

5

When he emerges from the room, he talks about depression.
The grandmother says constantly that the world is going to burn.
She can't stand it anymore, she doesn't want to continue living.
It is time for her to rejoin her two daughters.
Her two daughters, her two daughters, she repeats.
Before adding: it's all my fault.

Moridis prescribes tranquilizers.
He also insists: she must be watched day and night.
Never leave her alone.
Charlotte understands that this will be her role.
Who else could do it?
Her grandfather is a broken man.
He watches his wife struggling from afar.
And anyway, this is why Charlotte is here.

She came to look after them.
There has to be a price for finding refuge.
This is what he thinks under his long white beard.

Moridis wishes Charlotte *bon courage*.
As he's about to leave the house, he mentions her drawings.
I've heard, mademoiselle, that you are immensely talented.
News travels fast here.
They're just sketches, she stammers.
Drawings for children.
So what?
I would be interested in seeing what you do.
Charlotte is touched by his kindness.
She watches him go, toward other patients, other stories.

Charlotte is aware of the gravity of the situation.
She thinks they must create a sort of electroshock.
In her opinion, they should leave the Ermitage.
Her grandparents have been dependent on Ottilie for too long.
Little by little, they have lost their independence.
Relations with their benefactress are deteriorating.
The situation is becoming oppressive.
Isn't it always that way?
We end up hating those who give us everything.
Financially, leaving is possible.
They still have a little money.
When they left Germany in 1933, they were able to sell their belongings.
Charlotte goes to Nice, in search of a place to live.
She finds it on Avenue Neuscheller, at number 2.
A house with a name: Villa Eugénie.

.   .   .

Ottilie also thinks it will do them good.
She admits that relations between them have been cooler for months.
She asks Charlotte to come see her, as often as possible.
To let her know how they are, and to paint in the garden too.
You mustn't forget to live for yourself, adds Ottilie.
To live for myself, Charlotte repeats to herself.

The day of the move, they pass some soldiers.
These are the last ones to head east.
The region has been emptied of its men.
The soldiers are waiting for a conflict that doesn't come.
Is this it, then, the much-heralded apocalypse?
Snow begins to fall, and all is calm.
You could almost forget that war has been declared.

Inside the house, the chaos starts more quickly.
The move has not changed anything.
The grandmother spends her hours on the edge of a precipice.
Rare are those moments when she finds a little respite.
Her desire is still to die.
Charlotte drew her during this period.
In the sketches, she is horribly thin.
Wrapped up in herself, as if to hide her body.
On the other hand, there are no drawings of the grandfather.
Lost, isolated from everyone, he is infernal.
He remembers the first years in Nice.
Everything was wonderful then.
He enrolled in the university and made some good friends.
What is left to him now?
Nothing.
His wife is crazy, the country is at war.

And he misses Germany so much.
This makes him irascible, abrupt, domineering.
He is constantly giving orders to Charlotte.
Without really knowing why.
He is like the general of a ghost army.

6

Charlotte has not heard from her family for months.
The silence is unbearable.
At last, she receives a letter from her father and Paula.
Ottilie brings it to her in Nice.
Immediately she scans it in search of a name: Alfred.
Maybe they will mention him?
Maybe she will find out how he is?
That is what matters most to her.
But no.
There's nothing.
No Alfred.
She reads the letter again.
He might be hiding between the commas.
No.
No, he isn't mentioned.
Nothing about him at all.
She doesn't know where he is.
Is he even alive?

So she takes the time to read the letter properly.
Paula wrote it.
She describes the last few months.
They wanted to join her in France, but it's become impossible.

An influential friend was able to provide them with fake papers.
They took a plane with him to Amsterdam.
They left everything behind.
They arrived in Holland empty-handed.
Thankfully, some of their friends were already there.
It's like a little Berlin family reunited far from home.
Paula tries not to mention their distress.
But Charlotte is able to read between the lines.
She sees her father, in a daze.
Resolving to flee like a criminal.
Terrified at every second.
The fear of arrest, of prison, of death.
In the camp, he saw the way they killed anyone who happened to pass by.

Charlotte has always known her father as a powerful man.
And her stepmother haloed in glory.
Do they feel relieved, at least?
And for how long?
At least they're together, thinks Charlotte.
How she wishes she could join them.
Her freedom no longer has any value in her eyes.
To her, surviving like this seems worse than anything.
The letter begins to cause her pain.
The words underline what she is missing.
It is the physical proof of her exclusion.

Her grandmother shows no interest in the missive.
She hears a few snatches of it.
And focuses on their flight, the fake papers.
They are going to die soon! she cries out suddenly.
You're completely crazy! her husband yells angrily.

Charlotte finds herself between the two of them.
She asks her grandfather to leave the room.
Charlotte tries to calm the old woman.
As she spouts her macabre prophecies.
They're going to die!
We're all going to die!
Charlotte speaks softly.
The way you might speak to a child who's woken from a nightmare.
Everything will be all right . . . they're far from the catastrophe now.
But she doesn't want to hear any of this.
Death is everywhere!
Everywhere!
We must die before death takes us!
She mutters a series of incomprehensible phrases.
Then gradually calms down.
Her insanity manifests itself in urges.
Chaotic comings and goings.
Exhausted by her excesses, she finally falls asleep.
Sleep is the only place where she seems protected from herself.

7

In the weeks that follow, Charlotte receives other letters.
These are the last instants of her family ties.
We are now in 1940.
War was declared almost six months ago.
It is still going on in silence.
The only sound is of something falling, in the bathroom.
Charlotte rushes over to see what's happened.
Her grandmother has locked herself in.

Charlotte bangs on the door, begs her to open it.
But there is nothing: no reaction at all.
She hears a series of gasps.
The spaces in between grow longer, the sounds less audible.
Charlotte screams.
Finally, she manages to force open the door.
Her grandmother is hanging from the end of a rope.

Charlotte only just manages to save her.
She grabs hold of the body and the two of them fall.
Then the grandfather arrives.
As usual, he yells.
What are you doing?
You have no right!
You have no right to leave us like that!
And what about you, Charlotte?!
What were you doing?!
You must be crazy to leave her alone like that!
If she dies, it will be your fault!
You are really not to be trusted, you imbecile!
Charlotte ignores these cutting words.
She has to lay her grandmother down on the bed: that is the priority.
She looks like she's unconscious, but she sits up.
And touches her neck with her fingers.
Charlotte stares at the mark left by the strangulation.
A vivid red circle.
Red that is now turning bluish black.
The grandmother walks toward the bedroom.
Pushing away Charlotte, who tries to help her.
You should have let me die, she says.
Charlotte replies tearfully: you're all I have.

8

For days on end, she watches over her grandmother.
Never leaves her alone.
Charlotte opens the bedroom shutters wide.
She tells her about the sky, the beauty of the sky.
Look, look at that clear blue.
Yes, says the grandmother.
And look at the flowering trees too.
The colors that are like promises.
Soon, we'll go for a walk by the sea.
Promise me we'll go, Charlotte begs her.
Her words are soothing, a softness that heals the wounds.
She holds her hand.

The grandfather is outraged by these moments of consolation.
He can't stand it anymore, but what exactly?
Charlotte does not understand him.
He paces excitedly about the room.
As if he can't contain his rage anymore.
And that's exactly what it is.
He talks to Charlotte in a crazy monologue.
I can't stand any more of these suicides!
I can't stand it anymore, do you hear?!

There was your grandmother's mother.
She tried to kill herself every day.
Every day, yes, for eight years!
And then, there was her brother.
People said he was unhappy because of his marriage.

But I could see that the madness had gotten hold of him.

He would start laughing for no apparent reason.

Your grandmother was so sad.

I would go to see him, the madman of the family, as people called him.

Until the day when he threw himself in the water.

And his only daughter killed herself with barbiturates!

With barbiturates!

For no reason whatsoever.

And then there's her uncle, let's not forget him!

Yes, your grandmother's uncle.

He threw himself out of the window!

And her sister . . . and her sister's husband!

Oh, I don't know anymore.

It's everywhere, everywhere.

I can't stand it anymore!

You understand?!

And her nephew too, more recently.

The only survivor of the family; you didn't know him.

But he lost his job in the laboratory, like all the Jews.

So he killed himself . . .

Suicide is a death I wouldn't wish on my enemy!

Poor man: I remember him.

He was so kind.

Never raised his voice.

And now he's rotting in a cemetery.

He's nothing but a pile of bones now!

. . .

And our daughters!

Our daughters!

. . .

You hear me?!

Our daughters!

. . .

Your aunt Charlotte.
My beloved girl.
Oh, I loved her so much.
She used to follow me around everywhere.
She was like my shadow.
She listened to me.
She would play at being a Greek statue, to please me.
And then.

Nothing.
All gone.

She threw herself in the river, at eighteen.

Just like that.
I couldn't.
We couldn't go to the funeral.
Or maybe they should have buried us too.
Your grandmother and me, we've been dead ever since.

And your mother.
She suffered so much.
Do you even realize?
It was her darling sister.
They were inseparable.
People used to compare them all the time.
Like they were two versions of the same girl.
She was devastated.
But it wasn't obvious.

She did all she could to be strong.
She redoubled her efforts.
For us, she played at being two girls at the same time.
Your mother was such a kind person.
She would sing in the evenings.
So solemn, and so beautiful.
And then, she married your father.
With his obsession for medicine.
Thankfully, you arrived.
A child: that's supposed to be what life is about.
My granddaughter.
You.
Charlotte.

The grandfather stops speaking for a moment.
His last words were spoken more softly.
Not all tragedies can be screamed out loud.
He looks Charlotte in the eye.

Once again, he starts to raise his voice.
It grows louder and louder.
You . . .
You . . . Charlotte!
CHARLOTTE!
You were such a beautiful baby.
So, why?
Why?

Your mother was all we had left.
Your mother, and you.
It wasn't possible to do that.

Everyone is killing themselves, but not your mother.
She couldn't.
It wasn't possible.
She threw herself out of the window.
In our house!
Do you hear me?!

And you, you were there, afterward.
It was painful to look at you.
We would turn away so we wouldn't have to see you.
I remember your face.
You were always waiting for her to return.
You used to watch the sky.
She had told you that she was going to be an angel.
But no.
She was caught by the demon.
And she killed herself.
Yes, your mother too.

And your grandmother . . . why?
She doesn't want to live anymore.
But what about me?
Does she ever think of me?
What will become of me?
Do you hear me?!

I can't stand it anymore.

No, I can't stand it.

Not anymore.

. . .

9

Charlotte runs off.

She doesn't listen to her grandfather's last words.

He is still yelling, begging her to stay.

She hurtles down Avenue Neuscheller.

Until reaching the junction with the tulips.

Where should she go?

She doesn't know.

She runs until she's out of breath.

Toward the sea.

It's the sole possible destination.

The only place she can go without seeing another human being.

She runs across the beach.

Enters the cold February sea, fully dressed.

She moves forward quickly.

Knees, waist, shoulders disappear.

She is not a good swimmer.

A few more yards, and she could let herself go.

Her wet clothes grow heavy.

Pull her into the depths.

The waves crash over her.

She swallows saltwater.

Eyes to the sky, she glimpses a face.

Her mother's.

Is it finally the long-awaited angel?

Appearing with such precision.

Is she going to die?

She drifts, and memories are rekindled.

She sees herself as a child, waiting.
How absurd, that story about the angel.
Rage takes hold of Charlotte.
And propels her toward the shore.
No, she will not die by drowning.

Breathless, exhausted, she lies down on the shingle.
Her entire life is based on a lie.
I hate them, they all betrayed me.
All of them.
All that time.
Everyone knew the truth.
Everyone except me! yells Charlotte.
Disordered syllables resonate within her.
She can no longer articulate sentences.
She can't find the words.
To express the devastation.
Of what she has just discovered.
Not once did she suspect.
Never, never, never.
She cannot use words.
Do the words even exist to express such vertigo?
She understands the strangeness that has always been inside her.
That excessive fear of abandonment.
The certainty of being rejected by everyone.
What should she do?
Cry, or die, or nothing?
She gets to her feet, then lets herself fall to the ground again.
A puppet dropped on the empty beach.
Night falls, but this time it is different.
Night falls only on her.

. . .

She shivers with cold.
And crawls over to the Promenade des Anglais.
Looking as if she's just swum to the shore.
Now she walks quickly.
Advances through the night.
A wet shadow coming to life.

She thinks her grandparents are waiting up for her.
But no, they're asleep, and what a strange vision it is.
The bedroom window is still open.
Allowing the moonlight to illuminate the edge of the bed.
The light is soft, even friendly.
The moment is such a contrast to recent days.
They look like sweet children.
Charlotte sits on a chair to watch them.
And falls asleep in turn, close to them.

10

A few days pass, in rediscovered calm.

Can hours be described as looking pale?
Even their gestures are silent.
The grandmother brushes Charlotte's hair.
Something she hasn't done for years.
And so they re-enter a period of happiness.
Charlotte is incapable of asking a single question.
Why did no one ever tell her?
Why?

No, she stays silent.
She does not want to hear their explanations.
Besides, what good would it do?

She prefers to savor these moments of respite.
It would seem that her grandmother is finally at peace.
Unless this is a strategy?
Intended to make her jailer lower her guard.
The grandmother remembers her own mother.
Her craziness was constant, so they could never leave her alone.
She was watched day and night, her own potential murderer.

Charlotte hopes that everything will be better now.
She is her grandmother's mother.
For weeks, she has protected her, reassured her, warmed her.
Something very strong unites them.
And so she lets herself be lulled by an illusion.
And falls asleep.
When she opens her eyes, there is no one there.
How could her grandmother have gotten up without waking her?
Usually, Charlotte is such a light sleeper.
She freed herself from the bed without the slightest sound.
As if vanishing into thin air.

At that moment, there is a terrible sound.
The muffled thud of an impact.
Understanding, Charlotte runs to the window.
The grandfather wakes up too.
With a gasp, suddenly fearful.
What?
What's happening? he shouts.

The panic in his voice is something rarely heard.
Just like Charlotte, he knows exactly what is happening.

From the apartment, they can't see anything.
The interior courtyard is a black space.
The radiant moon of recent days has gone.
They both cry out the grandmother's name.
Several times, but without any real hope.
Go, go quickly and fetch a candle! orders the grandfather.
Charlotte obeys, trembling.
The two of them walk slowly downstairs.
Inside the courtyard, a cool wind blows.
They must try to protect the flickering flame.
They move forward, inch by inch.
Charlotte, barefoot, feels liquid under her feet.
Holding the candle, she kneels down.
And discovers a trickle of blood.
She utters a cry, puts a hand to her mouth.
The grandfather leans down in turn.
And, for once, says nothing.

11

The body lies on a bed for three days.
Strangely, the grandmother seems almost unchanged by death.
She already looked like this for a long time before.

Charlotte cries constantly.
She cries the tears that her grandfather cannot.
With Dr. Moridis's help, they organize the funeral.

Ottilie takes care of all the expenses.
The ceremony takes place on the morning of March 8, 1940.
The refugee children from the Ermitage are there.
Which makes the moment a little less gloomy.
They are happy to see Charlotte again.
They surround her with great warmth.

The coffin sinks into the ground.
Everything appears so calm.
Only the grandfather's lucidity is disturbed.
Apparently he no longer knows who they are burying.
Then he pulls himself together.
He cannot remember a single day without his wife's presence.
Has he ever lived without her?

After the ceremony, Ottilie invites them to her house.
Charlotte and her grandfather prefer to go home.
They feel the need to be alone.
And walk slowly down the cemetery path.
Charlotte deciphers all those names that were once lives.
Her mind is filled with images she cannot grasp.
Suddenly the grandfather grunts, as if he's been shot.
The pain awakens, and puts him in a rage.
The same rage that led him to tell Charlotte everything.
Hateful words pour from his mouth.
Words, more words, set free.
Then he grabs the young woman by her sleeve.
What? she says, head lowered, exhausted by the tragedy.
Why is he grabbing her like that?
What does he want now?
He grips her so violently.

She wants to fight back, to push him away, but she lacks the strength.
You're asking me what? he screams.
You're asking me what?
Just look.
Look all around.
Seriously, what are you waiting for?

Why don't you just kill yourself too?

Part Seven

1

Charlotte informs her family of the grandmother's death.
Paula worries about her stepdaughter's mental state.
Every line in her letter seems filled with sorrow.
Even the commas appear adrift.
Paula tries to find the right words to send in reply.
But words no longer have any value.
They should simply be there, to hold her in their arms.
Charlotte is suffering physically from their absence.
She thought the separation would be temporary.
But it has been more than a year already.
With not even the faintest prospect of being reunited.

The reply Charlotte receives will be the last.
Never again will she hear from her father and Paula.
There is unease on the borders and they are closing.
All Germans living in France have been asked to declare themselves.
Although it is obvious that they are refugees.
All the same, they are associated with the enemy nation.
The French State decides to lock them up.
In June 1940, Charlotte and her grandfather find themselves on a train.
Headed to the Gurs camp, in the Pyrenees.
The camp was initially constructed for Spanish refugees.
What is going to happen to them?
Charlotte remembers her father's face when he came back from
    Sachsenhausen.

Around her, she sees distraught Germans.

The journey lasts for hours.

This adds to the anguish of not knowing what will happen next.

Is she going to die?

Not one woman in her family has escaped their morbid fate.

Thirteen years separate the death of her mother from that of her aunt.

And another thirteen passed between her mother's death and her
    grandmother's.

Yes, exactly the same time lapse.

And all three died in almost exactly the same way.

A leap into the void.

Death has three different ages.

The girl, the mother, the grandmother.

So no age is worth living.

In the train that rolls toward the camp, Charlotte makes a calculation.

$1940 + 13 = 1953$.

So 1953 will be the year of her suicide.

If she doesn't die before that.

2

On their arrival at the camp in Gurs, families are separated.

Her grandfather joins the group of men.

He seems to be the oldest of them all.

The doyen of the shadows.

Charlotte asks a gendarme to let him stay with her.

He is too old to be alone, and he's sick.

No, no, just go into the women's shelter.

This is an order, so she backs down.
The young man has a billy club, and a dog at his side.
She realizes that there is no place for reasoned arguments here.
She leaves her grandfather and joins the line of women.
Among them, there is Hannah Arendt.

In Gurs, Charlotte is struck by the absence of any vegetation.
It is a total extermination of greenness.
She has gone from a wildly fertile landscape to a lunar landscape.
She examines the place, in search of even the faintest color.
Something attacks her in her flesh.
Her relationship with the world becomes purely aesthetic.
She paints incessantly in her head.
Unknown to Charlotte, her work is already breathing inside her.

Ugliness contaminates every detail.
In the shelter, there are no beds, only piles of mattresses.
The sanitary conditions are appalling.
Each night, they hear the squeaking of rats.
They rub against the women's hollow cheeks.
But that is not the worst thing.
The worst thing is the man who marches.
He comes and goes in front of the building with his flashlight.
From inside, the women can see the thread of light.
The unbearable sign of his presence.
It can go on for more than an hour.
They all know that he will end up coming in.
And here he comes now.
He opens the door, blinding the prone women.
He ventures between the mattresses.

The dog sniffs and licks its prey.
Wagging its tail, a happy accomplice in domination.
More than ever, it feels itself man's best friend.

Every night, the guard enters like this.
It is his wonderful ritual.
He goes in search of a prisoner to rape.
If any of them put up a fight, he can simply shoot them.
Shaking with fear, they curl up in balls.
He stops next to one of them.
With his flashlight, he examines her face and body.
Before moving on to another one.
Their fear excites him even more.
Finally he chooses a redhead.
Get up and come with me.
She obeys.
And he leads her to another hut.

3

Several weeks pass this way.
Between torpor and terror.
All everyone talks about is the German attack.
The French army's incredibly swift defeat.
How is that even possible?
Charlotte is petrified by the news.
The Nazis are going to control the country to which she fled.
Her refuge has become her prison.
So there will never be any end to her wandering.

. . .

Thankfully, the South is not part of Occupied France.
It is designated a *free zone*.
But free for whom?
Not for her, apparently.
She is barely even allowed to visit her grandfather.
He spends most of his days lying on a pallet.
Scarily thin, he is close to collapse.
When he coughs, a thread of blood trickles from his mouth.
Often he does not recognize Charlotte.
She feels utterly lost.
She begs the guards for help.
Finally, this young woman's distress stirs the compassion of a nurse.
She says she will see what she can do.
These are not empty words.
The management finally decides to liberate them.

Does Charlotte start to hope again?
She tells her grandfather that the horror is coming to an end.
They will return to the Ermitage, and he'll be able to rest.
She takes his hand, and he likes that physical contact.
The next day, they leave the camp.
But public transport is no longer working.
They must make their own way there.
Walking hundreds of miles with a cantankerous, sick old man.
They cross the Pyrenees.
In the sweltering heat of July.

Two months later, Walter Benjamin will commit suicide.
On the other side of the mountain range.
There is a rumor that stateless people can no longer cross the border.
Benjamin feels sure he will soon be arrested.

Exhausted by years of wandering and fear, he collapses.
And poisons himself with morphine.

I think of his words, which sound like a goodbye.
There is happiness—such as could arouse envy in us—
only in the air we have breathed,
among people we could have talked to . . .
German geniuses are scattered all over the mountains.
Hannah Arendt will succeed in leaving Europe.
Charlotte had a deep love of Walter Benjamin.
She had read his books, and listened devotedly to his radio broadcasts.
One of his lines could have been an epigraph for Charlotte's work:
The true measure of life is memory.

4

On the road, they ask to rest at people's houses.
Most of the time, they are refused.
No one wants to shelter Germans.
Finally, a young refugee comes to their aid.
He too is originally from Berlin.
He knows a place where they can sleep.
On the path there, in the darkness, he pushes Charlotte into a ditch.
Her grandfather is resting on a bench and doesn't see any of this.
His granddaughter fights back with all her strength.
She scratches her assailant's face.
And he runs off, cursing her.
You don't know what the hell you want, you stupid bitch!
Charlotte rearranges her clothes.
And rejoins her grandfather without a word.

She is used to burying her pain.
Even the rawest and most immediate.
She knows better than anyone how to cover a wound.
So accustomed has she grown to suffering.

At last they find an inn that will accept them.
But there is only one bed in the room.
Charlotte says she will lie on the floor.
The grandfather insists they sleep together.
A granddaughter and her grandfather, he says: it's normal.
Has she understood him correctly?
Yes, he becomes more specific.
He encourages her to undress and come close to him.
The earth reels on its axis.
All points of reference are gone.
So she goes outside for some air.
And waits for him to fall asleep before returning to the bedroom.

She sits in a corner, hiding her face between her knees.
In order to find sleep, she goes through her memories.
They are the only place where tenderness remains.
She hears Paula's voice, feels Alfred's kisses.
Eyes closed, she travels through beauty.
Now a painting by Chagall appears.
She reconstructs it precisely, visualizing each detail.
For a long time, Charlotte strolls among the warm colors.
And finally she is able to fall asleep.

Charlotte knows she cannot continue her journey like this.
Not with her grandfather watching her body, her every gesture,
    like a hawk.

Thankfully, they are told about a bus that runs along the coast.
Two days later, they are in Nice.
Their arrival at the Ermitage is a cause for celebration.
Everyone is so relieved.
No one had heard anything.
Charlotte, worn out, goes off to bed.
Ottilie comes to see her a little later.
And touches a hand to her forehead.
Charlotte opens her eyes then.
And a tear runs down her cheek.
It is so rare for anyone to show such gentleness toward her.

Ottilie realizes that this girl needs help.
She knows her family history.
Charlotte seems unable to stop crying.
Months of tears are finally released.
Thankfully, she manages to fall back asleep.
But her breathing is irregular.
The American lady sees shadows on the girl's face.
Shadows moving over her.
She knows that the last few weeks have disoriented her.
Her grandmother's suicide, the revelation of her mother's.
Then the imprisonment and the long walk back.
Ottilie is deeply affected by this vision of a ruined life.
She wants to save her.
I must help her and heal her, she thinks.
Before it's too late.

5

On Ottilie's advice, Charlotte goes to see Dr. Moridis.
His office is located in the center of Villefranche-sur-Mer.
He receives patients in a room of his apartment.
Kika, his daughter, born in 1941, still lives in the same place.
She moved back here after her parents' death.
When I tried to get in touch with her, I could never have imagined this.
That she kept her father's office intact.

Thanks to her, I was able to walk through the décor of 1940.
To live inside my novel.
The plaque is still on the door.

DR G. MORIDIS
CONSULTATIONS FROM 1:30 TO 4

I stood there a moment, observing every detail.
Kika and her husband were so sweet.
The doctor's daughter cannot remember Charlotte.
But her father often mentioned her.
What did he say?
She answers immediately: my father said she was crazy.
This takes me by surprise.
Not that he said it, but that this should be the first word.
Then Kika adds: like all geniuses.
Yes, her father was certain that Charlotte was a genius.

Just like Ottilie, the doctor is overcome with passion for Charlotte.
Admiring, tender, or simply concerned, he played a major role.

Every time he went to the Ermitage, he would speak with her.
And he was a frequent visitor.
Because there was often a sick child among all the orphans.
Charlotte intrigued him; her sensitivity blew him away.
For Christmas, she drew greetings cards.
With pictures of children descending from heaven.
Or attempting to reach the moon.
Something in those drawings touched Moridis very deeply.
A combination of power and naivety.
It was, he thought, simply grace.

The doctor takes Charlotte's pulse, examines her.
He asks her questions about the camp in Gurs.
She responds with incomprehensible monosyllables.
He is horrified by the state she's in, but doesn't show it.
You need vitamins, he prefers to tell her.
She remains head down, silent.
Moridis seems to hesitate.
Charlotte, you must paint, he says at last.
She looks up at him.
He repeats: Charlotte, you must paint.

He says he has confidence in her, in her talent.
These are words of comfort, but also of expectation.
There is no question of her letting herself go.
If she is suffering, then she should express that pain.
What he says stirs her deeply.

Moridis continues.
He finds the right words.
He mentions all the drawings she's made that he loves.

She has too much beauty inside her not to share it.
Charlotte is still listening.
What he says echoes what she feels.
And then Alfred's face appears to her.
A vision that is more alive than ever.
She thinks about his final words, on the platform.
How could she have forgotten?
She must live so she can create.
Paint so she will not go crazy.

6

On the way back, she breathes deeply.
This day marks the birth of her work *Life? or Theater?*
As she walks, she thinks about images from her past.
To survive, she must paint her story.
That is the only way out.
She repeats this again and again.
She must bring the dead back to life.
When she thinks this, she stops.
Bring the dead back to life.
I must go even deeper into solitude.

Did she have to reach the edge of what is bearable?
To finally consider art as the only possibility of life.
What Moridis said, she already felt it.
In her flesh, but not in her consciousness.
As if the body was always one step ahead of the mind.
A revelation is the sudden understanding of what you already know.
It is the path taken by every artist.

That vague tunnel of hours or years.
That leads to the moment when you can finally say: it's now.

She wanted to die; now she starts to smile.
Nothing else will matter anymore.
Nothing else.
Very few works are created like that.
With such a degree of removal from the world.
Everything is clear.
She knows exactly what she must do.
There is no more hesitation in her hands.
She is going to paint her memories like a novel.
The drawings will be accompanied by long texts.
It is a story that will be read as well as looked at.
To paint and to write.
This combination is a way of expressing herself *entirely*.
Or let us say *totally*.
It is a world.

It meets Kandinsky's definition.
To create a work of art is to create a world.
He himself was subject to synesthesia.
That intuitive union of the senses.
Music guided his choice of colors.
Life? or Theater? is a conversation between sensations.
Painting, words, and music too.
A union of arts necessary for healing a wrecked life.
The choice that must be made in order to reconstruct the past.

And it is also a whirlwind of power and inventiveness.
What happens when you discover this work?

A major aesthetic emotion.
I have not stopped thinking about it since.
Her life has become my obsession.
I have pored over the places and the colors, in dreams and in reality.
And I have come to love all Charlotte's work.
But the essential one, in my eyes, is *Life? or Theater?*

It is a life put through the filter of creation.
To produce a distortion of the real.
The protagonists of her life become characters.
As in the theater, they are introduced at the beginning.
Alfred Wolfsohn appears as Amadeus Daberlohn.
The Salomon family becomes the Kann family.
Charlotte speaks about herself in the third person.
If all is real, this distancing seems necessary.
In order to achieve real freedom in the story.
So fantasy can burst forth more easily.

A total freedom that is found in its form.
Along with the drawings and the story, she adds musical directions.
The soundtrack to her work.
We travel in the company of Bach, Mahler, Schubert.
And of German popular songs.
She describes her work as *Singespiel.*
The equivalent of a piece to be sung.
Music, theater, and movies too.
Her compositions are inspired by Murnau and Lang.
All the influences of a life are there.
But they are forgotten in the sparkle of her individuality.
To form a unique, unprecedented style.

·   ·   ·

It is time to begin.
Charlotte provides the user instructions for her work.
The setting for her invention.
The creation of the following paintings is to be imagined as follows:
A person is sitting by the sea.
She is painting.
A tune suddenly enters her mind.
As she starts to hum it . . .
She notices that the tune exactly matches . . .
What she is trying to commit to paper.
A text forms in her head.
And she starts to sing the tune, with her own words.
Over and over again.
In a loud voice until the painting seems complete.

Finally, she describes her character's precise state of mind:
She must disappear for a time from the human surface,
And sacrifice everything for this,
To recreate herself from the depths of her world.

Disappear from the human surface.

7

To begin with, she is unable to concentrate.
In the Ermitage, the children run all over the place, wildly energetic.
Ottilie tells them they must not disturb Charlotte.
She does everything she can to help her.
Finds her some very good paper, when food is becoming hard to find.
She and Moridis form an inner circle, protecting the genius.

Her grandfather is not part of the circle.
On the contrary, he harasses her.
As soon as he appears, she flees with her easel.
He pursues her, shouting out: you're here to look after me!
I didn't bring you here to paint!
He gets worse and worse.
When he steals fruit, he accuses the children.
Charlotte has no choice but to leave.
She must protect herself to continue her work.

Not long ago, she made the acquaintance of Marthe Pécher.
The manager of a hotel named La Belle Aurore, in Saint-Jean-Cap-Ferrat.
Marthe decides to let Charlotte stay there for free.
Is she, too, persuaded of her genius?
It's highly likely.
She offers her a room for as long as she needs.
Room number 1.
Here, for nearly two years, Charlotte will create.
It's a first-floor room, but the hotel is on a hillside.
All she need do is go outside and she can see the sea.
I have always imagined that room as a paradise, a refuge.
In reality, it is more like a cell.
A feeling accentuated by the brick walls.

The hotel boss hears her protégée *singing* as she works.
Yes, that is the expression that she uses.
Charlotte sings as she paints.
The music that she mentions in the margins to accompany her drawings.

According to Marthe, Charlotte hardly ever goes out.
Entire days consecrated to work.

That is, surely, the true measure of her obsession.
She remembers every word Alfred uttered.
And reproduces his dizzying monologues.
Page after page, she draws his face hundreds of times.
Years after their separation, without any photographs.
Charlotte's creative apnea is ecstatic.
Like a total devotion to the past.
I walk around room number 1 under the gaze of the young receptionist.
Tissem—that's her name—tries to help me.
While finding me rather strange, I imagine.
As I stare rapturously at the wall of a shabby room.
I wanted to know if the hotel possessed any archives.
The manager never called me back.
His name is Marin, the French word for sailor.
Must one have a seafaring name to run this hotel?
And most important: will he put a plaque outside the room?
I don't know why I'm so obsessed by plaques.
First of all, the place needs restoring.
I could take care of it.
Do everything so that these walls, with all their memories, are respected.
Even more than memories, they were the immaterial witnesses of genius.

8

Reluctantly, Charlotte must sometimes go to Nice.
Her grandfather lives there on his own.
She finds him sitting on a chair, going over his memories.
During one visit, in the middle of summer 1942, she spots a poster.
A new law requires all Jews to present themselves to the authorities.
Back at La Belle Aurore, Charlotte questions Marthe.

What should she do?

Although in truth, her decision is already made.

She will go and declare herself.

Marthe asks her why: it's absurd.

Charlotte replies: it's the law.

On the day in question, she leaves for Nice.

There is a long line outside the prefecture.

This reassures her, all these other obedient people.

Everyone is well-dressed; couples hold hands.

It's a hot day, and they have to wait for a long time.

After a while, several buses park near the square.

The people in the line exchange looks.

They try to reassure each other.

After all, there is nothing to be worried about.

Charlotte thinks about the camp in Gurs.

What if this simple census was actually a mass arrest?

Nothing could be worse than going back there.

In Paris, so it's said, there has been a huge roundup of Jews.

But who here really knows the truth?

Who knows what's happening in Germany or Poland?

No one.

Charlotte has heard nothing more from her father and Paula.

It has been so long.

She no longer knows anything.

Are they alive at least?

And Alfred, her Amadeus.

He is too unsuited to life to have gotten out.

No.

She cannot believe he is dead.

It's not possible.

. . .

Gendarmes appear suddenly out of nowhere.
They have discreetly encircled the square.
No one can get away.
It's a trap: everything is clear now.
How could she have been so stupid?
She and all the others.
The whole world is hunting them.
Why would today be any different?

They are told to get aboard a bus.
People rush toward the police to ask them questions.
Where are we going?
What have we done?
Calm turns quickly to dread.
The police start acting more firmly.
While trying to avoid panic.
It's just a routine check.
There's nothing to worry about.
Come on, it's fine, just get on the bus.
We'll give you something to drink once you've all sat down.

Charlotte sits with the others.
In that moment, she thinks about *Life? or Theater?*
What if she doesn't come back?
What will become of her drawings?
She trusts Marthe.
She knows she will look after her work.
But all the same.
It's not finished.
It's nowhere near finished.
What on earth made her believe she had all the time in the world?

She is in exile, on the run.
A pariah.
If she gets out of this, she will complete her work.
As quickly as possible.
She cannot imagine it remaining unfinished.

A policeman walks down the aisle.
His gaze alights on Charlotte.
He stares at her with intensity.
Why?
What has she done?
Nothing.
Nothing: she tells herself she has done nothing at all.
So why?
Why does he keep staring at her like that?
Why?
Her heart is beating too fast.
She is going to faint.
Is everything all right, mademoiselle?
She is incapable of replying.
He puts a hand on her shoulder.
And tells her: it'll be okay.
He tries to reassure her.
This policeman has stopped next to Charlotte because he finds her pretty.

Stand up and follow me.
She is petrified.
She doesn't want to move.
Maybe he's a pervert.
Like the guy in Gurs, who raped a girl each night.
What else can it be?

Why else would he pick on her?
She is the only young woman on the bus.
He wants to rape her.
Yes, that's it.
What else can it be?
And yet, his face looks so gentle.
And he does not seem sure of himself at all.
Little drops of sweat appear on his forehead.
He insists: follow me, mademoiselle.
Then adds: please.
Charlotte no longer knows what to think.
She is slightly reassured by his youth, his politeness.
But she can't really trust anyone anymore.

She decides to stand up and follow him.
Once they have both left the bus, he tells her to walk.
A few yards later, they are out of earshot.
Go, he says.
Go quickly, and don't turn around.
Charlotte doesn't move, so he insists: go on, leave now!
She understands what is happening.
He is, quite simply, saving her life.
She doesn't know how to thank him.
In any case, she doesn't have time to find the right words.
She must hurry.
She starts to walk.
Slowly at first, then increasingly fast.
In a back alley, she finally turns around.
There is no one behind her.

9

Back at La Belle Aurore, everything changes.
Charlotte is more than ever aware of the urgency of her situation.
She must act: there is no time to lose.
Her drawings become even more alive.
On many pages, there is nothing but text.
She has to recount her family history.
Before it's too late.
Some drawings are more like sketches.
She is not painting, she is running.
This frenzy, seen in the second half of the work, is incredibly moving.
A work created on the edge of a precipice.
Reclusive, frightened, wasting away, Charlotte forgets herself, loses
    herself.
Until the end.

In a letter, she will write these concluding words:
I was all the characters in my play.
I learned to walk all the paths.
And in that way I became myself.

The last painting is startlingly powerful.
Charlotte draws herself looking out to sea.
We see her from behind.
On her body, she writes the title: *Life? or Theater?*
It is on herself that the work closes, a work whose subject is her life.

This image is strangely reminiscent of a photograph of Charlotte.
In the picture, she is painting on a hillside.

Overlooking the Mediterranean.
She looks disinterestedly at the camera.
As if the photographer caught her in a moment of contemplation.
Of the life she leads in fusion with nature.
Charlotte seems to merge into the grass.
Wonder-struck by the color of the sky.
In the face of this radiance, one thinks of Goethe's last words.
On the shore of death, he began yelling: more light!

To die, one needs a blinding light.

10

She spends hours arranging the drawings.
She must put the story in order.
Number the final paintings.
She adds the last musical indications.
The whole thing forms three parcels.
On which she writes: "Property of Mrs. Moore."
The work must go back to Ottilie.
If she ever has to flee, if she ever has to die.
For now, the priority is to protect her work at all costs.
To find it a safe home.

Charlotte puts the parcels inside a large suitcase.
She looks around her room one last time.
Filled with a very particular emotion.
A mixture of joy and melancholy.
Her accomplishment marks a temporary end to her obsessive life.
Emerging from a work, the external world appears anew.

It is dazzling, after months of introspection.
That sudden look up when one's eyes have been turned inward for so long.

The farewell hugs with Marthe last a long time.
Charlotte thanks her with all her heart.
It is time to leave.
So she starts her journey to Villefranche-sur-Mer.
On foot, carrying her suitcase.
Who might have seen Charlotte that day?
Walking with a life's work.

Almost two years after her last appointment, she goes back to see Moridis.
He is the only person she knows she can trust here.
Ottilie has returned to the United States.
She left France, driven out by the imminent danger.
Taking nine children with her in a large car.
Plus two goats and a pig.
Headed for Lisbon, where she would board an ocean liner.
Charlotte had wanted to be part of this escapade.
Please, don't leave me here, she begged.
But it was impossible.
Unlike the children, she needed a passport.
Resigned, she gave some drawings to Ottilie.
By way of goodbye.
The American lady thanked her warmly.
Telling her: *they're worth their weight in gold*.
This woman was so important for her.
A mother and a patron.
So Charlotte entrusts her with *Life? or Theater?*, with Moridis as a
    go-between.
And dedicates the work to her too.

. . .

Charlotte stands outside Moridis's office.
She rings the doorbell.
The doctor himself opens the door.
Ah . . . Charlotte, he says.
She does not respond.
She looks at him.
She hands him the suitcase.
Saying *it is my whole life.*

It is thanks to Moridis that we know these words.
IT IS MY WHOLE LIFE.
What does she mean exactly?
I am giving you a work that tells the whole story of my life.
Or: I am giving you a work as important as my life.
Or even: it is my whole life, because my life is over.
Does this mean she is going to die?
It is my WHOLE life.
There is something haunting about this phrase.
Every possibility seems true.

Moridis does not open the suitcase.
He carefully puts it away.
One might even say: he hides it.
His daughter showed me the place where the work was protected.
I stood motionless staring at this so-real past.
An emotion of a rare intensity.
It is my whole life.

Part Eight

1

Charlotte goes back to live at the Ermitage.
Again, she thinks of her grandmother in the garden.
This no longer exists.
Again, she sees all the children running.
This no longer exists either.
They have almost all gone.
The house itself seems like an orphan.
And the beauty too has grown sad.

A man lives here now.
Alexander Nagler.
An Austrian refugee who was Ottilie's lover.
Though no one seems to know that.
Tall and clumsy, he doesn't say much.
What happens when two silent people meet?
Charlotte is unsure how to act.
Ottilie has left her *a friend*.
More specifically: *a friend I don't know what to do with*.
These are Charlotte's words.

Gradually they become used to each other.
Nagler is almost forty.
In 1939, fleeing the Nazis, he crossed the Alps.
A long, difficult crossing, which left its mark on him.
Though he appears strong, Alexander is very fragile.

A childhood accident means he cannot walk properly.
There is a huge scar on his forehead.
He is a sort of strange combination.
The kind of man who looks like a protector.
And whom you end up protecting.

Charlotte finds him too tall.
She doesn't like having to lift her head every time she talks to him.
Not that she does talk to him very much.
They pass each other in the garden.
Smile at each other or ignore each other.
But in November, everything changes.
Germany invades the rest of France.
So the two refugees mingle their fears.
They draw closer, and even begin to brush against each other.

2

Charlotte continues to visit her grandfather.
It's the same old story every time.
As soon as he sees her, he screams horrors at her.
And she ends up leaving, devastated.
He is the only family that remains to her.
Alexander reassures her.
Sometimes, he goes with her.
Of course, the grandfather cannot stand this new intruder.
When he is alone with Charlotte, he interrogates her.
Don't tell me you like that Austrian?
I forbid you to be with him!
Do you hear me?!

He's a bum!
Don't forget that we are Grunwalds!
You should marry someone of your own rank!

Charlotte finds him ridiculous.
He lives in the illusion of a world that no longer exists.
But she doesn't want to upset him.
She listens, no matter what he says.
This is how she was raised: to be docile with her elders.
That bourgeois education is a relic of the past.
And relics should be treasured.
We should do all we can to preserve them.
Through this absurd submission, Charlotte is able to touch her childhood.

She says yes to her grandfather.
And anyway, she doesn't love Alexander.
She likes him a lot.
She needs him, needs his warmth.
But that is not love.
She loves only one man.
Always the same man.
Did he even exist?

A few days later, the grandfather feels a sharp pain.
He leaves the house and walks toward the pharmacy.
He finally reaches it, but collapses just outside.
And dies like that, in the street.
When she hears the news, Charlotte feels relieved.
It's a weight off her shoulders.
So many times, she has wished he would die.
Would she have done something to bring forward his due date?

Later, in a letter, she will admit that she poisoned him.
Is this the truth?
Is it theater?
It is, at the same time, improbable and plausible.
If we consider all he put her through.
His incessant hostility and his contempt for her work.
And the sexual pressure too.

I exchange messages with Charlotte's disciples.
Particularly with Dana Plays, Ottilie's great-niece.
We discuss this option.
We fantasize about the possibility of this extreme act.
It is a novel within the novel.

Charlotte contemplates her grandfather's gravestone.
Which is also her grandmother's.
The two of them reunited forever.
Those connoisseurs of old rocks and dust.
The cemetery has been empty for hours.
Do people visit the dead less often during wartime?
Charlotte finally leaves, turning around one last time.
The way we do sometimes when we are walking away from the living.

3

Since November 11, 1942, France has been completely occupied.
The former free zone is now shared between Germans and Italians.
The Alpes-Maritimes department reports to Italian forces.
The Italians do not enforce the same racial policy as their allies.
Many Jews move to Nice and the region around it.

It has become almost the only accessible refuge in Europe.
Here, Charlotte and Alexander seem protected.
But for how long?

They talk constantly about the progress of the war.
Will the Americans land?
Charlotte cannot bear this speculation anymore.
Since 1933, they have been hoping for a better future.
And things have been getting worse and worse.
She desperately wants to believe in the Liberation.
But she won't until the American flag is flying here.

Their conversations are full of silences.
Words are scattered here and there in disorder.
Is that why they kiss?
To end the silence?
Neither of them is capable of taking the first step.
So how does it happen?
Gradually.
It is not a sudden urge.
But a sort of painstaking, methodical advance.
They speak to each other, sitting closer and closer.
Until one night their lips touch.

Charlotte is now a twenty-six-year-old woman.
In April, she celebrates her birthday with Alexander.
He found a little frame in a junk store.
And put one of Charlotte's drawings inside it.
She is moved by this gift, simple and beautiful.

It has been years since anyone touched her.
She hardly even remembers having been a woman.

The moments when Alfred would kneel down to embrace her.

When a man desired her, took her, roughly.

What has become of those instants?

Without knowing why, she is disgusted by something in her own desire.

She does not allow the advance of tender urges.

Alexander's caresses seem almost like attacks.

She pushes him away.

What is going on?

She can't respond.

He thinks it's his fault, wants to disappear on the spot.

How could he suspect that she too feels desire?

Unconsciously, she forbids herself anything that feels like a longing.

This does not last, and she lets herself go.

The instant is too intoxicating.

Charlotte takes Alexander's hand, and guides it.

His huge hand, uncertain but powerful.

She sighs immediately.

4

Making love becomes their main occupation.

The overgrown garden accompanies these sensual wanderings.

The trees, the heat and the scents.

It is the ideal theater for abandonment.

It feels, surely, like the birth of a world.

This period begins to overwhelm Charlotte.

She feels dizzy.

A different kind of dizziness.

So, is that it?

She moves her hand over her belly.
Stands there motionless, stunned.
She did not think this could happen.
She has often compared her body to a rampart.
The only weapon she has to protect herself.
And yet it seems that life has infiltrated it.
Yes, she is pregnant.

Alexander is ecstatic.
He walks on his hands in the garden.
If only the world were as simple as him.
He does not really understand Charlotte's reaction.
She would like to tell him that it is possible to be happy and lost at
    the same time.
That dismay is not incompatible with delight.
She thinks constantly about her mother.
Feelings she thought she had forgotten surge back.

Isn't it wonderful? says Alexander.
. . .

She just needs a little time.
The time to welcome joy.
The time to realize that she can have a happy life.
With a man and a child.
Isn't it wonderful? says Alexander again.
Yes, it's wonderful.

They spend hours discussing names.
Charlotte is certain it will be a girl.
Nina, Anaïs, Erika.

They anticipate life.

The future becomes a tangible space.

But for Alexander, there is something urgent they must do.

He wants them to get married.

I have my values, he says proudly.

He must wed this woman who is pregnant with his child.

5

Moridis and his wife are the witnesses to the wedding.

And here, you can feel the full force of that word, *witness*.

Charlotte and Alexander need witnesses to be certain that all this is
    real.

To make love official.

To declare it openly in a world where they must hide themselves away.

In the mayor's office, they give their identities and their address.

In order to be able to marry Charlotte, Alexander declares himself a Jew.

Whereas before this he had fake papers.

Why do they do this?

Surely because a moment arrives when not existing becomes unbearable.

For a long time I believed that this wedding led them to their downfall.

When I reconstructed the evidence, it all seemed to fit.

But I was to discover a completely different version of the story.

In fact, this wedding did not alter their fate at all.

It cannot be considered part of a social rebellion.

The proof: Charlotte and Alexander remained at the Ermitage.

Where everyone knew they could be found.

They feel safe, protected by the Italian presence.

That must be it.
Safe to the point of marrying, and giving their address.

In reality, though, the situation is precarious.
Some people try to help Jews flee the country.
The most ambitious initiative comes from Angelo Donati.
An Italian politician who draws up rescue plans.
He has meetings at the Vatican and with ambassadors.
And charters a fleet of ships that would be able to leave for Palestine.
The Italian consul general supports Donati.
The anti-Jewish laws are all overturned.
The Italian *carabinieri* protect the synagogue.
To prevent a raid by the French militia.
In Nice, Donati is also helped by Father Marie-Benoît.
Together, these forces form a protective bubble, united.
No doubt encouraging the newlyweds' recklessness.

But, on September 8, 1943, Italy surrenders.
And the Germans take control of the region.

6

The Jews must and will pay.
To ensure this, the Germans send one of the highest-ranking SS officers.
And also perhaps the cruelest: Alois Brunner.
His biography is sickening.
He is a small man with dark, frizzy hair.
A puny specimen with a twisted-looking body.
One shoulder lower than the other.

His embarrassment at not conforming to the Aryan ideal deepens his hatred.

More than anyone else, he has to prove that his blood is pure.

Unfortunately for him, he is a thoroughly unremarkable man.

He has no charisma, his voice doesn't carry.

And yet, once you have seen him, you cannot forget him.

The testimonies about his violence and depravity are enlightening.

Brutal and vulgar, he always wears gloves.

Because he fears physical contact with a Jew.

*

After the war, he manages to escape.

Changing his identity, he moves to Syria, where he is given protection.

The El-Assad family goes into business with him.

And makes the most of his skills as a torturer.

Finally he is unmasked.

International arrest warrants are issued.

But the Syrian regime will always refuse to extradite him.

Mossad agents dream of taking him like they took Eichmann.

Of abducting Brunner so he can be judged in Israel.

But it seems impossible to infiltrate Damas.

All they manage to do is send letter bombs.

Brunner loses an eye, and the fingers of one hand.

This does not prevent him leading a pleasant, peaceful life.

In 1987, a journalist from the *Chicago Sun-Times* obtains an interview.

About the exterminated Jews, Brunner declares:

"All of them deserved to die.

Because they were the Devil's agents and human garbage."

Before adding: "I have no regrets and I would do it again."

Brunner probably died in the mid-1990s.

Protected until his final breath.

*

Buoyed by his success in Greece and Drancy, Brunner heads for Nice.
He sets up his headquarters in the Hotel Excelsior.
Close to the train station, where he can pen up Jews before their deportation.
There is a commemorative plaque outside the hotel now.
The interior courtyard is impenetrable, acting as a sort of prison.
Encircled by buildings.
From their apartments, certain inhabitants have a front-row seat.
Spectators to executions.
Brunner no doubt found this idea exciting.
Having an audience to admire his barbarism.

He organizes a team of fourteen people.
A sort of commando unit for hunting Jews.
He thinks he will simply have to go to the prefecture, and everything will
    be simple.
But the prefect, Chaigneau, has destroyed the administrative lists.
He tells Brunner that the Italians took everything with them when they left.
It is the perfect lie, impossible to verify.
In this way, Chaigneau saves thousands of lives.
Furious, Brunner begins his hunt.
Some flee, attempting to cross the mountains into Italy.
Were Alexander not handicapped, perhaps they too would have gone.
But he cannot walk for that long.
And besides, Charlotte is four months pregnant.
So they decide to remain in hiding at the Ermitage.
The house is so large, no one will notice their presence.
Brunner promises a generous reward for any information.
From the very next morning, the letters start pouring in at his hotel.
Mass denunciation letters.
They are back in business.

They must flush out their prey in the early morning, when they are still in bed.
Old men stand wild-eyed in their pajamas in the Excelsior's courtyard.
Some of the arrested women are forced to undergo a physical assessment.
The good-looking ones are immediately sterilized.
And sent to the East as prostitutes for the soldiers.
But it's not enough, not enough, not enough.
Brunner always wants more.
He carries out interrogations with a singular brutality.
Forcing each prisoner to inform on family members.
Every Jew counts.
He finds out that a famous writer is living in a hotel in the region.
This is Tristan Bernard, who is nearly eighty years old.
At the hotel reception, there are protests, howls of outrage.
It makes no difference: the writer and his wife are taken away.
Sent first to Nice, then Drancy.
Where he will be liberated only due to the intervention of Guitry and Arletty.

7

In Greece, Brunner succeeded in deporting nearly 50,000 Jews.
Here, for all his efforts, he is well short of his target.
He has made barely a thousand arrests.
Thankfully, the letters continue to pour in.
There are still good French people, ready to serve.

It is the morning of September 21, 1943.
Not a letter this time, but a telephone call.

A young woman . . .
A German Jew, says the voice.

In Villefranche-sur-Mer . . .

. . .

In a house called the Ermitage.

The Er . . . what?

The Ermitage.

Okay, got it.

Excellent.

Have a good day, and thanks again.

Oh, you're welcome, just doing my duty.

One denunciation among many.

So that's all it is.

A denunciation for no particular reason.

Or maybe there is a reason.

But what?

Charlotte and Alexander are not bothering anyone.

They live as hermits.

Does someone hope to take over the house?

No, that's ridiculous.

No one took possession of the Ermitage.

So what, then?

There is no reason.

This is what is known as a gratuitous act.

Dr. Moridis's daughter Kika brings up the arrest.

Seventy years after the event.

She tells me what her father told her.

Suddenly, she is interrupted by her husband.

Some people know who denounced Charlotte Salomon, he says.

I sit there in shock.

I question him, and he goes into more detail.

DAVID FOENKINOS

These things get talked about.
In the towns, in the villages.
That's how it is.

I was not expecting this.
I don't know what to think.
It's an old woman who told people, he says.
Well, there's no way of knowing for sure.
She's a bit senile now.
And who knows, she may have just made it up.

I can't believe this.
Who would make up such a thing?

In Villefranche-sur-Mer, there are people who know.
So many years later, people are still whispering.
For years, the guilty ones lived here.
Just like they lived everywhere else.
There is no expiration date on denunciation.
But it remains buried.
Even today, no one will say what everyone knows.

Since then, I have often thought about this.
Should I have pursued my investigation?
Found the son or daughter of whoever denounced Charlotte?
To what end?
Is it really that important?

198

8

At nightfall, the truck enters Villefranche-sur-Mer.
And stops in the middle of the town center, outside the pharmacy.
Two Germans get out to ask directions.
And are given them, precisely, politely.
Thanking their hosts, they leave, delighted to receive such a friendly
    welcome.
Might the informer have been deliberately vague in the address they gave?
Arranging things so they could quickly warn Charlotte that the Germans
    were after her.
Were they frightened or were they willing collaborators?
Charlotte has lived here for years.
Everyone knows her.
So what went on in the head of the person who gave directions?
After all, she is a bit strange, that girl.
She doesn't talk much.
You don't really know what she's thinking.
No, seriously.
A little interrogation won't do her any harm.
At worst, they'll drive off with her somewhere.

Headlights off, the truck comes to a halt soundlessly.
Two men enter on each side of the garden.
Charlotte is just coming out of the house.
She looks up and sees the soldiers.
They rush at her, grab her by the arms.
She screams at the top of her voice.
She struggles, tries to get away.

One of the Germans violently yanks her hair.
And punches her in the gut.
She tells them she's pregnant, begs for mercy.
Please, leave me in peace.
This makes no difference to them.

As the soldiers are trying to subdue her, Alexander comes out into the
    garden.
He wants to intercede, to take Charlotte back from enemy hands.
But what can he do against a rifle?
They threaten him and he takes a few steps back, leans against the wall.
They tell Charlotte she must pack a few belongings.
Head down, she doesn't respond.
One of the Germans pushes her toward the house.
Her legs cannot move, and she falls in the grass.
They brutally yank her to her feet.
Alexander wants to do something, but there is still a gun pointed at him.
He realizes they are going to take her away.
Only her.
They are not interested in him.
It's unbelievable.
He can't let her go, with their child.
No.
So he looks at one of the soldiers and yells:
You have to take me too: I'm Jewish!

Charlotte and Alexander walk upstairs.
They must pack some clothes.
She wants to take a book, but they won't allow it.
Just clothes and a blanket, and hurry up.
A few minutes later, they are sitting in the back of the truck.

The vehicle speeds away into the night.
Brunner will be happy.

9

They are crammed into the hotel courtyard, along with other arrested
    Jews.
The most terrifying rumors circulate.
They hear screams, sometimes gunshots.
Brunner's torture chamber is located next to his bedroom.
Sometimes he gets up in the middle of the night to piss on a Jew.
From his window, he can see the prisoners.
He takes pleasure in watching their fear and despair.
But at the same time he knows he must do all he can to reassure them.
The peacefulness of the transfers depends on it.
No one must guess the next stage of the program.
They must avoid hysteria and desperate acts of bravery.

Brunner himself comes to speak to them.
He puts on his most affable voice.
Though this is the same voice that screams at people before killing them
    in cold blood.
He admits that he sometimes loses his temper with the more obstinate
    prisoners.
But he wishes them no harm.
If everyone plays their part, there will be no trouble.
He tells them about a Jewish state that has just been created, in Poland.
We will give you receipts for your money.
It will be returned to you once you are there.
The community in Krakow will help you settle down.

Everyone will find a job that suits them.
Who really believes this?
Maybe all of them.
After all, Charlotte's father returned from the camps.
She herself was liberated from Gurs.
They must not give up hope.

Early in the morning on the fifth day, they have to leave.
They walk to the station, where a train awaits them.
The French police help the Germans, taking care of logistics.
This is a convoy of several hundred people.
Once they are inside the train, nothing happens.
Why cram them all inside if they are not going anywhere?
They are waiting for Brunner to give the green light.
Maybe he simply wants to prolong his pleasure.
They begin to feel thirsty, to struggle for breath.
Alexander tells them his wife is pregnant.
So they do their best to give her some space.
So she can sit down, with her knees in her face.
No one can hear, but she sings to herself.
A German lullaby from her childhood.
Finally the train starts moving, and a breath of air enters the carriage.

10

On September 27, 1943, they arrive at Drancy.
Alexander and Charlotte are immediately separated.
This is a transit camp.
Death's waiting room.

11

On October 7, at four in the morning, they must be ready.
Each deportee must write their name on their luggage.
Still the illusion of a future home.
In order to reduce panic to a minimum, families are reunited.
At last Charlotte is back with her husband, who is already in a much
 weakened state.

On the platform, she notices certain men.
They are dressed as if for a wedding.
Elegant, standing upright, holding their suitcases.
Wearing hats that they might remove if a woman passes by.
She does not see even the slightest hint of hysteria.
It is a form of civility amid the ruin.
Whatever happens, do not show the enemy your true devastation.
Do not offer him the pleasure of a torture victim's face.

They are convoy number 60.
Seventy people are crammed into a carriage designed to sit forty.
With all their luggage too, of course.
Inside the carriage, there are old people and lunatics taken from the
 asylums.
Who can really believe this will be a labor camp?
Why would they take the insane and the dying?
This clue does not escape them.
One young man says: they're going to kill us, we have to get out of here.
He tries to find a means of escape, wants to smash the floorboards.
Several people grab him to stop him doing this.

The Germans were very clear on this point.
If a single person is discovered missing, everyone in the carriage will
    be executed.

Time passes slowly.
Or rather, in truth, time does not pass.
Strangely, glimmers of hope appear here and there.
In very rare and brief instants.
Charlotte thinks she will be reunited with her family.
Maybe even Alfred is already there.
How will he react when he sees her married and pregnant?
To her surprise, it is her father she misses most.
All those years without any news.
Alexander is no longer able to reassure her.
Hour by hour, he is breaking down.
An ulcer gnaws at his stomach.
He looks almost transparent.
Some voices say: you must be in good health.
When you arrive, stand up straight.
Pinch your cheeks so they have some color.
The labor camp will take only the strong ones.
But how can anyone look strong after three days in these conditions?

Charlotte and Alexander support each other as best they can.
At each stop, he fights to get her some water.
She is so afraid that the baby will die.
Sometimes she can't feel it move anymore.
And then, suddenly, there is a quiver, a kick.
As if the baby, too, is already learning to save its strength.
Beginning its life as a survivor.

12

At last the train reaches its destination.
The night is black and icy cold.
As at the start of the journey, the carriages remain closed.
Why don't they open the doors?
Why don't they let them breathe?
They must wait for daybreak.
This lasts more than two hours.

Finally the deportees emerge from the train.
Distraught, exhausted, starving.
In the morning mist, they cannot see the camp.
They cannot even see the dogs that bark at them.
All they can see is a sign above the entrance gates.
Arbeit Macht Frei.
Work makes you free.

Now they must line up in rows.
Alexander and Charlotte know that they are going to be separated
    again.
They savor their final moments together.
Soon, they will be told which group they must join.
Some will be spared from an instant death.
Because this convoy has arrived the day after Yom Kippur.
When the Nazis gassed a few more Jews than usual.
As if to mark the occasion.
So there are lots of free places in the shelters.

. . .

The line moves slowly forward.
What should they do?
What are the right responses?
Charlotte wants to explain that they have made a mistake.
She is not Jewish.
Can't they see she isn't Jewish?
And she's also five months pregnant.
They must let her get some rest in a private hospital.
They're not going to leave her like this.

Now it is her turn.

In the end, she says nothing.
A man speaks to her without even looking at her.
He asks for her last name and first name.
Her date of birth.
Then he asks what job she does.
She replies: draftswoman.

He looks up at her, contemptuous.

What the hell is that?

I'm a painter, she says.

Staring at her, he finally notices that she's pregnant.
He asks her if she's expecting a baby.
She nods.
The man is neither pleasant nor unpleasant.
He simply notes the information down.

And bangs the stamp down on her form.
Then he indicates to Charlotte the group she must join.
A group with lots of women, essentially.
She walks forward slowly, carrying her suitcase.
Shooting regular glances toward Alexander.

Now it is his turn.
It is over more quickly than hers.
He is told to join the group opposite his wife's.
He looks for her as he walks.
When he sees her, he gives a little wave.
A few yards later, he is swallowed up by the mist.
Charlotte loses him.

Less than three months later, he will die of exhaustion.

13

On the wall of the building is a sign that says everyone must take a
    shower.
Before entering the shower room, they all get undressed.
They must hang their clothes on a hook.
A guard yells at them.
Whatever you do, don't forget the number of your coatrack.
The women memorize this last number.
And enter the vast room.
Some hold hands.
The doors are then double-locked, as in a prison.

•   •   •

Naked under the cold light, the bodies appear gaunt.
Charlotte and her belly stand out.
Amid the others, she does not move.
She seems to remove herself from the moment.

To be here.

Epilogue

In May 1943, Paula and Albert are arrested in Holland.
Working as nurse's aids, they survive the camp in Westerbork.
Albert is asked to sterilize Jewish women.
Especially those from mixed marriages.
He refuses categorically, then changes his mind.
He says he needs to return to Amsterdam with Paula, his assistant.
To pick up the necessary instruments.
They take advantage of this opportunity to flee.
And go into hiding until the end of the war.

Once peace returns, they try to find out what has happened to Charlotte.
After months of uncertainty, they learn of her death.
Devastated, Paula and Albert blame themselves.
They should never have sent her to France.

In 1947, they decide to follow her footsteps.
To see the places she spent her final years.
They find Ottilie Moore, who has returned to the Ermitage.
The American tells them about her memories of Charlotte.
How things unfolded.
The grandmother's suicide.
The grandfather's reign of terror.
And then the marriage with Alexander.
Vittoria, the cook, is also there.
She is the one who prepared the wedding meal.

She describes the menu in great detail.
And the atmosphere at that beautiful celebration.
Was Charlotte happy? her father asks.
Yes, I think so, Vittoria replies.
At that moment, no one dares tell them that Charlotte was pregnant.
They will learn this later.

Another important witness joins them.
It is Dr. Moridis.
He seems deeply moved at the idea of meeting Paula and Albert.
He talks about wonderful moments spent with Charlotte.
He avoids mentioning his concerns about her mental health.
Consultations when he doubted her lucidity.
I admired her so much, he adds.
His voice trembling with emotion.

A few months before this, he had handed the suitcase to Ottilie.
Now that lady goes off to find it.
Moridis repeats the phrase Charlotte said to him: it is my whole life.
A life in the form of a work of art.
Albert and Paula discover *Life? or Theater?*
It's a terrible shock.

They hear their little girl's voice.
She is there, with them.
Their Lotte, lost to them years ago.
Thanks to her, the memories breathe again.
It is *their* whole life too.
For hours, they pore over the drawings.
They have become characters.
It is proof that they have lived.

2

They return to Amsterdam, their new hometown.
After hesitating for a long time, Ottilie gives them the work.
They spend whole evenings analyzing it.
Some parts make them laugh, others offend them.
It is Charlotte's truth.
An artistic truth.
They could never have suspected all the thoughts in her head.
And especially not her extravagant love for Alfred.
Later, Paula will say that it could not have been anything more than
    a fantasy.
According to her, Charlotte and Alfred can't have seen each other more
    than three times.
She does not seem to believe that they might have met in secret.

That is the whole beauty of Charlotte's project.
What is life?
What is theater?
Who can know the truth?

And years pass like that.

In Holland, Paula finds old friends from the world of culture.
She begins to sing again, and life starts over.
From time to time, they show the drawings to visitors.
People are always moved and amazed.
An art connoisseur tells them they should organize an exhibition.

Why did they never think of that before?
It would be a fabulous tribute.

This takes time, and they must also prepare the catalog.
Charlotte's work will finally be exhibited in 1961.

It is a considerable success.
Beyond the emotional impact, her work fascinates through its
    inventiveness.
Through the total originality of its form.
And its eye-catching warm colors.
Charlotte's reputation immediately starts to spread.
In the years that follow, several other exhibitions take place.
In Europe, even in the United States.
Life? or Theater? is published as a book.
It is translated into several languages.
Paula and Albert are interviewed on television.
Though they appear embarrassed on camera, they speak very movingly
    about Charlotte.
They tell her story.
She is alive, through their words.
A team of reporters travels to the South of France.
Witnesses speak, such as Marthe Pécher.
No one seems very surprised to be questioned about Charlotte.
More than twenty years after they knew her.
As if everyone had already guessed that she would become famous.

But the work's fame does not last as long as it should.
The retrospectives become less frequent.
Until finally they are rare, too rare, unjustly rare.
Albert and Paula grow old and unable to take care of Charlotte's legacy.

In 1971, they decide to bequeath everything to the Jewish Historical
    Museum in Amsterdam.
The collection is still there, though not as a permanent exhibition.
Most of the time, it is kept in the basement.
In 1976, Albert dies.
Much later, in 2000, Paula joins him.
They are buried together in a cemetery near Amsterdam.

3

And Alfred?

With help from one of his students, he manages to escape Germany.
In 1940, he moves to London, where he will remain for the rest of
    his life.

After the war, he gives lessons again.
Very quickly, his methods meet with great success.
People respect him, people listen to him, he exists.
He also starts writing, and publishes a novel.
Finally relieved of his angst, he lives through the 1950s.
No longer feeling like a dead man among the living.
The past seems distant to him now, perhaps nonexistent.
And he no longer wants to hear about Germany.

Thanks to some mutual friends, Paula finds out where he is.
She writes him a long, friendly letter.
What a pleasant surprise, after all this time.
In his reply, he begs her to sing again.
And repeats that she is the greatest.

But he does not mention Charlotte.
Because he fears the worst.

A few months later, he receives another letter.
Although, in fact, it is not a letter.
It is Charlotte's exhibition catalog.
There is also a pamphlet with a biographical note.
And so what he knew without knowing is confirmed.
She died in 1943.
He starts flicking through the pages of the book.
And quickly realizes how autobiographical it is.
He sees drawings of her childhood, her mother and the angels.
Then, Paula appears.
And . . .

Alfred discovers himself, suddenly.
One drawing.
Two drawings.
A hundred drawings.
Leafing through the book, he sees his face everywhere.
His face and his words.
All his theories.
All their conversations.
Never could he have imagined having had such an influence.
Charlotte seems obsessed by him, by their affair.
Alfred feels a shiver all over his body.
As if something had grabbed him by the back of the neck.

He lies down on the couch.
And remains there, prostrate, for several days.

• • •

One year later, in 1962, Alfred dies.
He is discovered fully dressed on his bed.
He looks like a man who is going on a journey.
As if he knew the time and date of his departure.
This gives him a wise appearance.
And even a form of serenity, which is rare for him.
The woman who finds him runs a hand over his suit.
And feels the shape of a document in a pocket.
An interior pocket, close to his heart.
She pulls the paper toward her.
And discovers an exhibition catalog.

For an artist named . . .

Charlotte Salomon.